My Dahlia
and Other Stories

My Dahlia and Other Stories

Tales from a Small Town

SHAMSUDDIN JAAFAR

PARTRIDGE
A Penguin Random House Company

To order additional copies of this book, contact
Toll Free 800 101 2657 (Singapore)
Toll Free 1 800 81 7340 (Malaysia)
orders.singapore@partridgepublishing.com

www.partridgepublishing.com/singapore

Contents

To
my wife, Sapiah,
my daughters, Nurhayati and Nurizzati,
and my sons, Afiq and Aiman.
Please forgive me.

My Dahlia

I have not met Pit for at least ten years. We would send text messages to each other on and off, festivity greetings mostly, always saying we should get together over tea, but we never did. Even when I do come back to my hometown, I would rather spend time with my parents and my brothers and sisters than meet with my old friends. I just feel that we no longer have anything in common.

"Why don't you take it to Pit's laundry?" Mother suggested when I showed her the black patch on my favourite pants. We were having a get-together to celebrate Mother's first grandchild by my eldest sister. Mother cooked her specialty and our favourite, fish-head curry. She used the biggest pot we had and cooked outside the house, using a traditional kerosene stove because the pot wouldn't fit on her kitchen cooker hob. I was assigned, after the cooking was done, to return the blackened pot to its shiny silver hue. I accomplished the task to Mother's satisfaction, but the pot had left streaks of black on my brown khakis. Putting water and soap on them only made it worse.

"Pit's laundry? Wow, that was so long ago. Is he still running it with his father?" I asked Mother.

"No. I heard they all migrated to Australia. It seems that his sister, the one who was studying there, got married to a

Mat Salleh, and they all moved there. Pit stayed here. I don't know why. Theirs is a strange family," Mother said.

That evening, after we'd had our fill of Mother's curry and the new addition to our family started bawling her little heart out for some private time with her mother, I drove out to town to find Pit's laundry shop. Mother said it hadn't moved from its original location, but the roads had changed. Every road was a one-way street now.

The row of shop houses, one of which was Pit's laundry, still maintained its British colonial facade, although the businesses occupying its premises were all very different from what I remembered. The coffee shop where Pit and I used to have charcoal-toasted bread with margarine and kaya (coconut spread) and the "four-digit-numbers prediction agent's" shop were not there anymore. Instead, the whole three-storey block was now a boutique hotel, with one half of the ground floor converted into its reception lobby. Pit's shop was exactly next to the lobby area, and next to his laundry was a fast-food restaurant that occupied the rest of the block.

Even Pit's shop had been upgraded, to the extent that if Mother had not said it was still here, I would not have recognised it. I remember it used to be shared with a dressmaker's shop, with open frontage. You could literally throw your bag of laundry to Pit from the roadside as he sat behind the counter, waiting for customers. Now it occupied the whole lot. (Pit told me later that the dressmaker died, and because none of her offspring had learned how to make dresses, her children agreed to let out her half until the deceased's estate was sorted out, and then they would sell it to Pit. Pit hadn't heard from them since, but he diligently posted a cheque to one of her sons on the first of every month.) A glass wall and front door with magnetic lock kept the unwanted out and the air-conditioned ambience in. I peered inside and saw a computer and printer on a shiny Formica-laminated front countertop. Near the door handle, above the "pull" sign, a box was stuck to the glass door with a small button. On top of that was a note that said "press for service." I did and heard a bell ring somewhere in the back of the shop. A few minutes later, a woman emerged from between rows of clothes that hung on a laundry conveyer. She reached beneath the counter, and the glass door clacked open. I pushed the door; it resisted. Then I pulled, as the door instructed. I walked in, a little embarrassed. She smiled and asked what she could do for me. She had an Indonesian accent.

I asked her if she could get the black patch out of my pants, and she said, "Of course." She took my pants, folded them in half, and dropped them into a basket. After she gave me the ticket, I asked her if Pit was around. She went to the back and called out, "Boss! Customer wants to see you!"

Pit was surprised to see me. He opened the small door at one end of the counter separating us and ushered me to the back of his shop. He hugged me, punched my arms, and said I looked fatter now. In the back, we sat at a square foldable table on red plastic chairs. I supposed it was where he did his administrative work, based on the calculator and files on it,

and also where he took his meals, based on the plastic plate
and cup, and utensils neatly arranged at one side of the table.
He asked his assistant to make some tea. We reminisced,
laughed, and teased each other, especially about both of us
being single at our "advanced" ages. (I was twenty-eight, and
he was twenty-nine.) I asked about our other friends, Lan
and Mat. These two had been part of our small-town gang,
but they were a year younger than me. Both, according to
Pit, were now earning their living in Kuala Lumpur. Mat
would be getting married in December. We talked for a long
time, in between Pit tending to his customers, until closing
time. We shook hands and gave each other another hug. I
went off as he and his assistant stayed on to lock up. All that
time, *she* never crossed my mind.

Maybe it was the news I heard on the radio on my way home
that evening. A new-born was found dead in a toilet at a
factory somewhere. The police caught the eighteen-year-old
mother, who led them to her nineteen-year-old lover. That
reminded me of Dahlia. It reminded me of us.

*****

I never thought that any kind of relationship would bloom
between Dahlia and me, even though Pit and I had been
friends for as long as I can remember. In hindsight, I realised
that Pit had made every effort to distance me, Lan, and
Mat from his little sister. But I did steal a glance or two at
her when the gang and I were hanging around Pit's house,
usually after school.

"My ugly sister" was how Pit would differentiate her from his other younger sister. And her shyness made her unapproachable.

The first time I spoke to her was when Pit invited us to sleep over at his house because his parents had gone away to Kuala Lumpur to send his older little sister off to Australia to continue her studies. We made burgers, fried french fries, and boiled instant noodles, creating a mess in the kitchen. Then we watched porn in the living room. Pit had rented a few tapes, but I got bored after the first one and went to the kitchen to get a cold drink. Dahlia startled me. I had assumed that there was nobody else in the house. She was cleaning up; her back was to me as she was washing the pan and the spatula we had used to fry the burger patties. She only turned her head slightly when I came through the kitchen door and then totally ignored me.

I went to the fridge to get ice and reached for the jug of plain water on the dinner table. The kitchen wasn't very big, and underneath the lingering smell of fried beef patties, I thought I could smell her. It's that certain smell girls have.

I sipped my drink, leaning against the fridge, and studied Dahlia's profile. I saw the pupils of her eyes darting towards me every few seconds as she hurried to put the pan and spatula away. The kitchen was clean, just as it had been before we ravaged through it.

"How come you didn't go to KL?" I asked as she was leaving the kitchen.

"I have something on at school tomorrow," said she as she slipped out the swinging kitchen door and up the stairs. Her voice surprised me. It occurred to me that was the first time in my life I had actually heard her speak. I had always imagined that she would have one of those squeaky, geeky voices, but she had a normal voice, a nice voice.

I finished my drink, put the glass in the sink, and started to walk out to rejoin my friends. Then I turned around, washed the glass, and put it away on the rack. The guys were sitting on the carpet playing poker, using toothpicks as betting chips. In the background were the sounds coming from the porno movie that no one was paying attention to. I stopped the VCR and switched off the TV.

"Hey, I was watching that!" Pit said.

"No you weren't. And besides, your sister's here, bro. Why the hell didn't you tell us?" I said.

"What?" Mat and Lan said in unison.

"So what? She's so damn bloody shy; she's locked herself in her room," Pit said.

"She was just down here. She cleaned up the kitchen."

"Why, that stupid girl," said Pit, as he got up from his lotus position and went upstairs. We heard him bang on a door and call out his sister's name.

"Lia! Open this door!" we heard him shout. We heard the door open and then slam shut, followed by shouts and the sound of a slap. Lia gave out a little cry, and the door opened and slammed shut again.

When he came down stairs again, I told Pit that he didn't have to hit his sister. Pit said to mind my own business. I told him to go to hell and was about to head for the door. But Pit caught my hand and begged me to stay. He apologised and said he had told his sister not to come down, but she was so stubborn. We knew Pit was just venting his anger at Dahlia because he was losing at poker. He was a sore loser.

We stayed on for another half hour or so. Lan switched the TV back on and pressed play on the VCR. The porno started to look the same, so we couldn't tell if we had seen it already. The cigarettes we smoked were making us sick. Nobody felt like continuing the abandoned poker game. What Pit did to Dahlia had spoiled the mood. It was almost two in the morning by then. Mat and Lan said they wanted to go home. I too decided to leave with them. But then Pit pleaded that I accompany him for the night.

"Why? Are you scared?" I asked.

"No! Of course not! I just need the company, OK?" he said.

We laid out the cushions from the rattan sofa on the floor to sleep on in the living room, switched off the lights, and talked for a while until I heard Pit snoring. I kept thinking about Dahlia. I even had a thought of going upstairs to check on her. I wondered if she was OK. But I must have dozed off too.

Pit woke me up. He was scrambling around trying to clean up the mess we had made. He picked up the cushions and put them back on the rattan sofa, readjusted the coffee table, and mumbled to himself that he was late. He was supposed to open the shop at nine every day. It's already eight when he woke me, and he had to send Dahlia to school for netball practice. I volunteered to send her if Pit would lend me his father's motorcycle, but Pit said "no need" and herded me out of the house.

I took a shower as soon as I got home. I ate some toast and cold tea left over from the breakfast Mother made, and I decided to go to my school – my ex-school, rather, since at that time I had just finished my SPM[1] exams and was working in my father's law firm as an office boy while waiting for the exam results.

I stood in the shade of a huge Angsana tree, squinting into the morning sun at a group of girls playing netball in the distance, on the other side of the running track. I was trying to pick out Dahlia. But outside her home, Dahlia wore a headscarf, and there were a few girls wearing them on the court.

---

[1]   SPM is equivalent to the O-Level and is the second last public examination at the secondary school level before the entry into a tertiary level education at a university or other higher education institution.

It was a Sunday, and there weren't any other people in the school except the group of girls on and around the netball court.

"What are you doing here?!" said a voice behind me.

"Eh … Cikgu, I, err –"

"Peeping at the girls, are you?" said Cikgu Zakaria, the sports and physical education teacher.

"Yes, err, I mean, no, Cikgu. I'm looking for somebody," I stammered.

"Hey, aren't you –" Cikgu Zakaria peered upwards at me as if examining my nostrils. His forehead wrinkled as he tried to think where he had seen me before. Cikgu Zakaria should know me. I had been on the school football team that won the national inter-school tournament two years ago, and he had been our team manager.

"Yes, Cikgu, I am. How are you, Cikgu?" I said, holding out my hand. Cikgu Zakaria took it and shook it once. Then he tightened his grip.

"Then you have no business here – what *are* you doing here?" he said, looking up at me. He was rather short, but he had such an overpowering personality that the principal had made him the disciplinary teacher. We nicknamed him "Yoda."

"I'm looking for Dahlia, Cikgu," I said, grimacing.

"What did you do to her?" Cikgu Zakaria tightened his grip even more.

"Ahhhh! Cikgu, that hurts. I didn't do anything to her … ahhh!" was all I could manage. Cikgu Zakaria let go of my hand.

"Why are you looking for her? Are you two having an affair? She's too young; you're too young. What is the matter with you? Go to college, get a degree, get a job – then you guys can think of sex. What's wrong with you kids today?" Cikgu Zakaria rambled on.

I was rubbing my hands, which were still throbbing from Cikgu Zakaria's vice-like grip. "I'm not having an affair with her, Cikgu. I'm just a little … concerned."

"What happened? She did not turn up for practice today. Is she sick? Just what I need. The tournament starts in two weeks, and we've lost our best shooter," grumbled Zakaria.

"She's not here?" I asked, disappointed.

"No. I called her house, and her brother said she's not well. But I think he's lying. I don't trust that brother of hers. Do you know what's going on?" Cikgu Zakaria looked genuinely worried.

"I'm not sure, Cikgu," I said. There was a long pause. Both of us were looking at the girls practicing in the distance.

"Cikgu, I need your help. Can we go to Dahlia's house to check on her? I have a bad feeling."

Cikgu Zakaria nodded. Then he walked across to the girls and shouted at them that practice was over for the day. I could hear moans and complaints from the girls.

*****

Cikgu Zakaria rang the bell and waited. No one opened the door. Cikgu Zakaria pressed the button on the left pillar of the front gate again. We both could hear the muted *ding-dong* from inside the house. I looked up at the upper windows and thought I saw the curtains of one of the windows move.

"Nobody home?" Cikgu Zakaria seemed to be asking the question to himself.

"Hey, what do you think you're doing?" he yelled in a whisper when he saw me climbing over the gate and jumping into the compound of Dahlia's house. I ignored him.

"Lia!" I shouted. "I know you're inside! We just want to talk. Please."

Dahlia's house was a linked house, and my shouting attracted the attention of the immediate neighbours. A woman from next door stuck her head out of her front door, looking at me and then at Cikgu Zakaria outside the gate.

"Er, we're from her school," Cikgu Zakaria said to the lady with an apologetic smile, and she disappeared back into her house.

The door finally opened, and Dahlia stood in the gap, clearly indicating I was not welcomed. There was a bruise on her left cheek. A little cut was on her lower lip, which she was trying to hide by sticking her tongue out over it.

"Pit's not here," was all she said. I just stood there under the porch, looking at her, and I found myself admiring her. How lovely her eyes were. They were brown.

"Are you OK?"

"Yes." She lowered her eyes when she realised I was staring into them.

"Cikgu Yoda was worried. Why didn't you come to practice?"

"I didn't feel like it." Her answer was short, but I saw a gentle smile break on her face when she heard me referring to her netball coach as Yoda.

"Oi! What's going on there? Dahlia, are you OK? Are you sick?" Cikgu Zakaria called out from outside the gate. He was shielding his eyes from the sun.

Dahlia stepped out of the house and walked past me to unlock the gate. I took a deep breath, inhaling her scent. "Come in, Cikgu, please. Sorry to keep you standing in the heat."

I believe that day was the day that I fell in love with her. She invited both of us in and served us iced rose syrup drinks in the kitchen. I sat quietly, looking at her "plainness." But it was her demeanour, her quiet confidence, her honesty, and her total lack of pretentiousness that attracted me most. It was as if she had accepted her "ugliness" and was not out to impress anyone. She was oblivious of how lovely she was. She was different from all the other girls I had known.

"Did you brother did that to you?" Cikgu Zakaria asked.

"Yes," Dahlia answered.

We waited, but she offered no further explanation.

"It was your fault, right?" Cikgu probed.

"If being an adopted child is a fault, then yes," she said unemotionally.

"Adopted?" I was surprised.

"Yes, she's adopted," Cikgu Zakaria confirmed.

*****

Dahlia's house was just on the next street from mine. And after that day, when we had a long and enlightening conversation, I started to spend more time with Pit at his house. On days when I was not photocopying something or sending out documents to my father's clients, I would always come around to Pit's house, even when I knew he was not around. I just wanted to catch a glimpse of Dahlia.

That day, in the kitchen with her and Cikgu Zakaria, I was the least talkative. The two of them were talking about netball, the team, her exams, the other teachers, and her friends. They laughed, and I laughed, although, for the most part of the conversation, I had no idea what they were talking about.

I sat there at the dining table, sipping my rose syrup, taking in Dahlia. The way she talked, her smile, her skin, her hair, her neck, her hands – they were perfect. Her voice, the way she laughed, and the way she darted glances at me as she was talking to Cikgu Zakaria, enthralled me so, that I could not look away from her. She knew I was staring at her, but she carried on with her conversation with Cikgu Zakaria as if I hadn't been there.

I learned that day that she was adopted, and that was the very reason Pit did not want her to come out of her room. It was wrong for her to be in the same room with him and the three of us, because we were not her *mahram*[2]. Pit was really being protective. On any other occasion, her (adopted) parents would have insisted that she come with them, but she did not want to miss her netball practice. Pit apologised to her in the morning and offered to send her to school, but

---

[2]   In Islamic legal terminology, a *mahram* is an unmarriageable kin with whom sexual intercourse would be considered incestuous, a punishable taboo.

she refused. Pit had to go and open their laundry shop, so he left her alone.

I couldn't get her out of my mind. A week after the kitchen meeting, I wrote her a letter. I rode my bicycle to her house, rang the bell, and waited, hoping that she would open the door. I knew Pit would be at the shop, and her father hardly ever answered the door, so it would be either her mother or her. It felt like a long time passed, and I was just about to ring the bell one more time when the door opened and out came Dahlia's lovely, plain head.

"Pit's at the shop," she said.

"Er … Lia, I have something here," I said just as she was about to retract her head back into the house.

"What?" she said.

I threaded the envelope containing my first-ever love letter through the bars of her house gate and waved it a little.

"What?" she said, still at her door.

I shook the envelope again. Lia refused to come. "What?" was all she said.

"Can you please take this letter?" I said, a little annoyed.

She came out, took the letter, turned around, and went back into the house.

"Dear Dahlia," I wrote. "Last night I could not sleep. I do not know why, but I have been thinking about you a lot. I am not an emotional person, but somehow while talking to you in the kitchen together with Yoda, I saw a side of you that I never knew existed. Being so close to you, almost touching you, made my heart beat faster. Now I crave the sight of you every day. Many people will say that we are too young, but Dahlia, I will take a chance and say that I do believe I have fallen in love with you.

"Please do not tell your brother.

"ILY4Ever."

I imagined that she would be laughing her head off after reading my letter, and I believed that this was true when for almost a week I did not get any kind of response from her. During this time, I would still come by to see Pit at his house, hoping to get a glimpse of Dahlia. But when she did appear or when we passed each other, she would not even look at me. She walked past without acknowledging my existence.

Then Lan came by on his way back home from school and gave me a letter. He said it was from some girl in another class; he nudged and winked at me and teased me about having a secret admirer. But he did not hang around to find out who it was. He said he was too hungry, and his mother had cooked his favourite food that day.

"Dear Sam," the letter started. "Your letter caught me by surprise. I never expected that I could have such impact on anyone, much less on one of my brother's macho friends. I must admit that I have admired you from afar, and I must confess that you were the reason I came down that night, incurring the wrath of my overprotective (adopted) brother.

"I took my time to answer your letter because I am not sure that you really are who or what you say you are and that what you have written is truly from your heart. I may be young, but I really believe that I am a very good judge of character.

"I have seen you, and I think your feelings are genuine. I do not know if this feeling I have for you is love, for I have never had such feelings toward anyone before. I know I love my father, and I love my mother. But what I feel for you, I don't know how to describe. I, too, crave the sight of you. And yes, my heart skips a beat each time you are near. And I am so very happy each time I hear your voice in the front yard calling out my brother's name. How I wish it was my name instead.

"I hesitate to reply to your letter because I do not know how to proceed from here. Do we continue in our present way? Do we openly declare our feelings? Do we dare to go against all that will oppose this relationship because we are too young?

"I am a very emotional person, and I am afraid of what will become of us. What if we are destined not to be together after all that has been and will be said and done?

"I do not know what the future holds or what fate has planned for us, but for now, I can tell you that I too am in love with you.

"ILY4ever 2"

We continued to send each other secret messages. Usually, on my regular visits to Pit's house, I would place neatly folded notes under a particular vase in Pit's living room and check to see if anything was there for me the following day. It was rather cumbersome, but we got away with it every time. Nobody suspected that there was something going on between me and Dahlia, not even to the present day.

Our letters were mostly saying how we missed each other and how we wished we could be together. We even touched on the subjects of marriage and raising a family. Sometimes, when nobody was looking, we would brush against each other while passing. That would make my day.

Our affair started in early January. In July, I was offered a place in Westminster University in London. I told Dahlia about this, and she was visibly upset at the thought of being far away from me. A week before the day of my departure, she was totally moody. She spent most of the time in her bedroom, coming out only to go to school and to eat. I too was a little distraught, especially during her self-imposed curfew. She did not leave any notes under the vase, despite me having written to her almost every day.

I was to leave for Kuala Lumpur on a Monday, two days before my flight to England. On the Saturday before that, I went around to Lan, Mat, and finally to Pit's houses to bid them good-bye. As I was sitting in the living room with Pit and his parents, Dahlia came downstairs. She looked at me and then to the vase. She asked her parents if they should invite me to have some tea in the dining area. She volunteered to make some. They all agreed. When the tea was ready, she called her parents. As all of us were adjourning to the dining table, I managed to discreetly walk past the vase and pretended to accidentally brush against it, almost knocking it over. I caught the vase in one hand and grabbed the small note underneath it with the other.

Afterwards, we said our good-byes. Pit hugged me, saying he'd miss me terribly and making me promise to write. At that time, I caught a glimpse of Dahlia peeking from the upper flight of the stairs.

I rushed home to read her letter. It was the shortest note I ever received from her.

"Dearest Sam," she wrote. "Meet me at school after netball practice."

*****

That was about ten years ago. After my meeting with Pit at his shop, I could not sleep. I kept thinking of Dahlia. The next morning, I bade good-bye to my parents and, before driving back to KL, took a detour and dropped by Pit's shop. I wondered how I could ask about Dahlia without raising some suspicion in Pit's mind. I needed to know about Dahlia. Was she still here? Was she now working in KL or some other city? Was she studying in our local universities, or had she flown away to a foreign country?

Pit was surprised that I showed up again. He thought we had already said our good-byes yesterday. My pants would only be ready the next day, as promised, and Pit had said he would personally deliver them to my parents' house after closing time. "Do you want to pick up your pants today?" he said. I could see the slight wariness on his face and in his speech.

I gave out a nervous laugh. "No, no," I replied, shaking my palm at him. "Pit, I need to ask you something."

Pit smiled one of those *I-knew-there-was-something* smiles. He looked at me for a while before replying, "Anything, my friend." He then opened the small door in the front counter to let me in. He asked if I wanted anything to drink, and I said no.

We sat at the table, and I decided just to get to the point. "Pit," I started. "Where's your sister Dahlia? What's she doing now?".

He had never expected that. There was a pause before his answer. "She's not here," Pit said, looking at me with a solemn face. He was suspicious. Why wouldn't he be? He had always been suspicious of everybody who asked about Dahlia – more so now, I suppose, especially from me.

I waited for a bit more elaboration than the obvious answer Pit had given, but nothing else came out of his mouth. "Not here? Where is she? She should be about twenty-four or twenty-five now."

"Twenty-four this year," Pit said, and that was all.

"Come on, Pit. I want to know more. What's she doing now? Studying? Working?"

"What's this all about, Sam? Why are you so curious about her? Was there anything going on between you – oh my God, there was, wasn't there?" Pit looked at me with both his hands cupping his mouth.

I told Pit about Dahlia and me. I told him I went looking for her at school and ended up falling head over heels over her while she, Yoda, and I were having a conversation in the kitchen. And I told him that we had sent each other notes under the vase.

Pit gave out a sigh and shook his head. He had a little smile on his face when I mentioned the vase, apparently amused to learn of all this a decade after it had happened under his nose.

There was a long silence. "Is that all, Sam? Tell me all, Sam. Are you telling me everything? Was it really just an innocent young love?" Pit kept his stare upon me.

I looked back at him and suddenly felt nervous. I saw anger in his eyes. Was I responsible for something? I was, it seemed – something I would soon learn. Something that might bring an end to my newly rekindled friendship with Pit.

"She got pregnant, Sam," Pit said quickly.

"Oh my God, I … I … oh my God," was all I could say.

*****

I remember that day. It was a hot Sunday afternoon, but there was a breeze blowing. I remembered thinking how nice it would be to lie in a hammock under a tree. I felt a tinge of melancholy as I rode my bicycle to school to meet Dahlia. I thought, *This is the last time I will be seeing all this. Tomorrow, I will be gone from here.*

The school was deserted. I slipped through the small pedestrian gate next to the big gate and cautiously walked past the guard room, ducking under the window.

"Hey." Dahlia startled me from behind.

"Where's the guard?" I wondered.

"Oh, he went to buy himself lunch," she said casually.

"Doesn't he usually bring his own food from home? He's not supposed to leave the school unguarded."

"I know. That's why I'm here. I'm hanging around here while he buys his lunch," Dahlia said with a smile. "OK, actually, I gave him money so he could get a nice lunch," she finally confessed.

"Why?" I asked.

"Do you think we can meet here if the guard is around?" she said practically.

"Oh yeah, then let's get out of the sun and disappear before the guard comes back," I said, suddenly feeling the sting of the afternoon heat on my head.

"Come," Dahlia said, taking my hand. I held on to hers and squeezed it tightly, not knowing when I would have the chance to do so again.

She led me into the girls' dressing room. I was a little nervous, but I wanted to be with Dahlia. She closed the door behind her and immediately turned toward me and wrapped her hands around my neck. I was shocked, but I reacted by putting my hands around her body. It felt wonderfully good. She smelled wonderful. We stayed that way for a while. Then she let go of my neck, cupped my face and pulled it to her, and planted a kiss on my lips. Her lips were soft and sweet, but I pulled my head back out of guilt.

"What's wrong?" she asked.

"Err, have you done this before? Err, I mean …"

"I know what you mean. No, this is my first time too. But I know what to do. I've watched those tapes that Pit often rents," she said and planted another kiss on me. Then I felt her hands unbuttoning and unzipping my jeans.

I will always remember that day. I had just turned eighteen a month earlier. She was barely fifteen. I will always remember that day: the day we lost our innocence.

*****

"So it was you," Pit said softly.

"We wrote each other. I was her supposed pen-pal, Samantha," I confessed. "But she stopped writing after a couple of months. She never replied to any of my letters. I thought she was busy with her exams. I even asked my mother about you and your family, and she said she doesn't know. She said she hadn't seen any of your family for a long time, except you. I was heartbroken, Pit. Really, I loved her. But when she went quiet, when she didn't reply my letters, I assumed she had moved on," I said. Tears were welling in my eyes, and my throat felt dry and constricted. I was expecting him to get up from his chair, grab me by my collar from across the table with one hand, and start pounding my face with his other hand. That would be the Pit I knew.

But I saw the anger left his face. And I thought I saw relief, perhaps from knowing the truth at last. "She never revealed to us who the father was." Pit said with a sigh. "She didn't know she was pregnant. She started to have morning sickness, and we took her to see a doctor. The doctor broke it to my parents that she was having a baby.

"We pressed her for the truth, but she just kept mum. I suggested an abortion; she refused and threatened to kill herself. My parents, after a long discussion, decided they did not want the pregnancy aborted either. She quit school, and we told the teachers that she was having some health complications that required her to take a long break. One of my father's friends was a doctor. He wrote a medical note that Lia was not fit to go to school for a year due to some complicated medical condition.

"After the baby was born, my mother went to register the baby as hers. We had help from my father's high level contacts at the National Registry. Then my parents and Lia moved to Kuala Lumpur. My parents bought an apartment there, which was intended to be rented out. They stayed there for a few years. Lia went to a private school. Then my other little sister said she fell in love with some Australian guy. They got married there, and she became a citizen. My parents and Lia and the baby went to attend the wedding, but they ended up staying there. My new brother-in-law has good connections with the Australian immigration department."

"How come you didn't go with them?" I asked.

Pit cried. I saw his eyes well with tears. He wiped them away with the knuckle of his right index finger. "Do you know, my father actually asked if I was the father? He beat me up to a pulp until I shit in my pants, literally. Dahlia kept screaming it wasn't me, but he kept hitting me. I ran away for a few days, slept at mosques, and begged food from Lan or Mat. I guess Lia must have convinced my parents, somehow, that it couldn't have been me. My mother came looking for me and took me home."

Pit stopped for a while to regain his composure. "God knows, I did all I could to protect her. I never looked at her in any other way except as my little sister. I got beat up for that. Father stopped speaking to me. He's never one to say sorry, even when he knows he's in the wrong. And I ... I guess I've never forgiven him. When they wanted to move to KL, my father wanted to sell the laundry business. I told my mother I wanted to stay here and run the business."

"I am so sorry, Pit. Oh my God, I am so sorry. I didn't know. Why didn't she write to me and tell me about all this?" I wondered.

"What if she had? What would you have done? Come home and admit to statutory rape? Would you abandon your studies, your lifetime ambition, just to be with her? She said it was destiny. She was an illegitimate child too, you know. Father found her in a box one morning while he was jogging by a mosque. He took her home, and Mother thought she was too beautiful to give away. So she managed to get a birth certificate for her. We told her the truth when she was twelve, to explain why she couldn't be alone in the house with me."

"Where is she now?" I asked.

"Perth, with your son."

Sue and Rocky

Faroukh, Rocky to his friends, stood in the shadow of the bus stop, out of the bright amber light of the street lamp and the headlights of oncoming vehicles. The tinkling and gurgling sound from the flowing waste water in the big monsoon drain behind the bus stop was mesmerising, bringing him back to his hometown far away in Bangladesh. He wondered what his wife was doing at that moment. He inhaled hard on his clove cigarette and watched sparks fly from the glowing end as it crackled and popped. Smoking was a filthy habit he had picked up here in Malaysia after befriending Muktar, the Indonesian man who ran the canteen at his workplace. Sudarseh was late, and if they missed the next bus, they won't be able to catch the eight o'clock show at the town cinema.

In the distance, he could hear the call for the dusk prayers from the village mosque. A Muslim by birth, he only prayed when it was convenient. This was the most appropriate time for him to meet Sudarseh, when the locals were mostly indoors, tending to the transition from their day to night lives. But Sudarseh's tardiness was the least of his worries. In this close-knit Malay community, his romantic liaison with a local woman could well cost him his life.

Rocky lived with fifteen of his compatriots in a house rented by his employer situated in this predominantly Malay village about fifteen kilometres from Muar, the second-largest city in the southern state of Johor, on the Malay Peninsula. Muar was located on a river that led into the Straits of Melaka and said to be one of the oldest settlements on Malaya. The word 'Muar' was derived from *Muara*, which means 'estuary'. Throughout history, Muar had been occupied by the Portuguese, colonised by the British, and attacked by the Japanese.

At present, as more and more factories were built in the outskirts of this town, the locals had learned to tolerate the presence of the immigrant workers like Rocky. But they maintained their trepidations and suspicions, despite the workers' having lived here for over a decade.

Rocky pondered the itinerary for tonight: movie, then dinner, then send her home. Then, ah. … he must control his urges.

The last time he had been intimate with a woman was more than a year ago, just before he left for Malaysia from Bangladesh. Though he had promised his wife celibacy, his libido was getting the better of him as the days passed. As a matter of principle, he convinced himself he would not seek the services of a prostitute. In reality, on outings with his fellow immigrants to the red-light areas in town, he found that the ones that attracted him he couldn't afford, and the ones he could afford repulsed him. Thus, he had so far been true to his vow of celibacy and faithfulness.

There was a girl whom the others called Sue, though, at the furniture factory where he worked. She was a rather tall, big-boned woman, probably in her thirties. She had Indian or Mid-Eastern blood in her veins, Rocky was sure. They passed each other on the factory floor every day, giving each other a smile but nothing beyond that.

Then one day, about three months ago, he came upon Sudarseh (her full name, as he later learned) stranded in this very bus stop, caught in heavy rain. She had just alighted from the factory bus and was wondering whether to brave the rain and run to her home some half a kilometre away or wait it out at this bus stop. She was wishing she had brought an umbrella when an express bus sped by and splashed a puddle over her.

Rocky was on his way back to his hostel, cycling hard against the rain and wind, when he saw Sue at the bus stop, which was situated at the junction that leads into the village. He had requested a leave of absence that day (all the workers were entitled to one day's leave a month) and was coming back from town after posting a letter to his wife and sending some money to her via telegraphic transfer.

As he approached the bus stop, Rocky climbed off his bicycle and ran, pushing his ride, to get under the shelter of the bus stop. This startled Sue, as she was checking the contents of her bag to see if any of her things had been drenched by that inconsiderate express bus. But whatever apprehensions she had towards the approaching figure turned to relief when she realised it was Faroukh, her co-worker. She had always had a certain admiration for Rocky. If he had been one foot taller, with a little bit more meat on the bones, she would have thought he looked like Salman Khan, Sudarseh's favourite Hindi film star, with his wet hair swept back. But a few of her friends thought he looked like Rowan Atkinson's Mr Bean.

Rocky and Sue just stood there, suddenly realizing they were lost for words. Rocky, under tremendous pressure to say something, blurted out, "Are you wet?" which he regretted. His grasp of the Malay language was enough to carry a conversation, but he could neither read nor write in Malay.

Sue let out a little laugh and covered her mouth with both hands, amused at the thought of how she was supposed to answer him. She kept silent instead and gave Rocky a little smile.

Thirty-one years old and still unmarried, Sue had given up all hope of finding the right man. Now she would take any man. Almost six feet tall, very tall for an Asian woman, and with an athletic build, she could be intimidating. She had sharp facial features, a legacy of her Arab and Javanese ancestry. She might not be exclusively categorised as beautiful, but some men did find her attractive, especially since she was well endowed in the bust area. Perhaps if she had been fairer she would have had more suitors.

There was once, when she was eighteen, a boy from a neighbouring village who took interest in her. But when her over-protective stepfather found out, his threats of bodily harm were so convincing that the boy left the village and was never seen again.

*****

Since that chance meeting, Rocky and Sue had been meeting here regularly on the days when they were assigned to the morning shift, which started at eight and ended at four, giving them time to rest and refresh themselves before going out on their dates.

Usually, on these dates, they would either catch a movie or eat dinner and walk along the riverfront. Dinner would be at a fast-food restaurant in town next to a budget hotel. Sue would almost always suggest that they eat there because there was also a small laundry in between the restaurant and the budget hotel where she liked to send her silk dresses (not that she had many of them) for dry cleaning.

Although Rocky fantasised of the time when he and Sue would consummate their relationship, he did not have the heart to force himself on her. But at least the woman he fantasised about was a real and accessible person. They started to hold hands – never openly, though – on the bus, when there wasn't many people, but mostly only in the cinema. At times, during the romantic or scary scenes, Rocky would put his arm around her broad shoulders. This, however, was not an easy task when your girlfriend was taller than you.

*****

It was a beautiful night. There was a slight breeze, and the sweet scent of freshly cut grass mixed with the smoky odour of burnt leaves. The moon shone, full and bright. It was close to midnight, and the village was deserted except for a lone figure sitting in an old, dilapidated car. He had parked strategically underneath a huge acacia tree, waiting. He had been there since about eleven thirty. Bent on discharging his thoughts about Sue's secret liaison, he waited for however long it would take.

As midnight approached, he saw in the distance two figures, one tall and one slightly shorter, walking slowly and holding hands under the bright silvery moonlight. They were silhouetted by the amber street light at the far end of the road.

Atan twisted the ignition key, and the car gave a horse-like braying sound as the engine stubbornly refused to start. This annoyed him, as he needed to ensure that he would get Rocky away from Sue as soon as possible. His annoyance drove him to keep twisting the ignition key until the engine finally burst into life and roared, as if in futile protest.

Atan put the car in gear and drove slowly forward towards the oncoming lovebirds. The car stopped next to the couple. Atan got out, one leg still in the car, and barked at the couple over the roof of the car.

"Hey, you devil, you illegal immigrant, I told you to stay away from her. Who do you think you are, Shah Rukh Khan?" Atan's voice rang in the cool midnight air.

"No, uncle, who do you think you are, Amitabh Bachchan?" asked Rocky, his voice low and stern. He was angry but still in control.

"Waaaahh … Very brave, ahh, you," said Atan. "Wah, very brave ah you?"

"What! You think I am afraid of you? You are nobody, not even her real father. *You* are the devil, Atan!" Rocky said, pointing a finger at Atan.

Upon being called the devil, Atan paused for a few moments. How much had Sue told him? "OK, let's settle this once and for all, you ungrateful immigrant. Come, let's settle this. We go to the old cemetery now. Are you man enough?"

"Rocky, no. Please, he'll kill you. You don't know my stepfather. Please, Rocky," pleaded Sue. She was holding on to Rocky's arm and pulling him away from Atan.

"No, Sue, you have suffered enough. Tonight, I free you from this monster. Come, Atan, you take me there in your old, stinky car. Let's see who the coward is. Let's see who is the real man," Farouk said.

"Sue, you go home!" Atan shouted at Sue, who was still hanging on to Rocky's arms. "Go home!"

"Don't worry, I'll be OK. You go home. Don't worry. I'll see you tomorrow. Tomorrow, we'll get married," Rocky said, just to spite Atan.

"What are you going to do, Rocky? Please," Sue cried.

"Don't worry; I will be OK … You go home. I'll see you tomorrow," assured Rocky.

She started to walk away slowly, looking over her shoulder a few times. Rocky got into the car with Atan, and they drove away.

The old cemetery was the original Muslim burial ground for the people of this village, but it had been deemed fully occupied a few years ago. Thereafter, the deceased were buried at the new cemetery about five kilometres away. Since even those who visited and kept up the old graves had passed on, the old cemetery became unkempt, with tall grass and creeper plants growing among the pointed little tombstones. It was actually quite near the main road, but thick undergrowth and ancient trees obscured it from view, although during the day, the hum of the traffic could be clearly heard.

When they reached the old cemetery, Rocky got out of the car, rolled up his sleeves, and marched on to a clearing between the tombstones. There he stood thinking that Atan was right behind him.

But he wasn't. Atan stayed in the car, gave a wave, laughed, and drove away. Rocky suddenly realised, even in the dim light of the midnight moon filtering through the foliage above him, that there were others at the cemetery.

*****

When Sue was twelve years old, Rojiah, her mother, had married her lover, Atan bin Senawi, three months after Sue's real father died. A carpet seller, Sue's real father was on the road most of the time. Rojiah was beautiful. She met Atan while she was waiting for a bus in town. Even with Sue in tow, Rojiah attracted the attention of many men, young and old alike. Rojiah was wallowing in her disappointment at having to go to town on her own to buy new school uniforms for Sue since the new school term would start soon. Her husband had promised they would make the trip together but, as on many other times, never fulfilled his promise.

Atan was bold enough to approach her, and Rojiah liked the attention. Their acquaintance progressed rapidly into intimacy.

Sue never liked Atan, but he was always around the house whenever her father was not. Often, before and a few months after her mother and Atan were married, she was left alone to play by herself when her mother and Atan locked themselves up in the bedroom for an hour or so. She never had any brothers or sisters. As a child, she used to be envious of her friends who had siblings, but eventually she became thankful that she was the only one to suffer the way she had.

Atan had presented himself as the sole heir of a wealthy businessman. In truth, he was the only child of a petrol kiosk owner. He never really worked a day in his life, but he lived the life of the rich as an only son does. To finance the wedding ceremony (since Rojiah insisted on a major reception), Atan stole money from his father. Eventually, the crime was uncovered when Atan short-changed his accomplice, the kiosk attendant-cum-cashier, who then did the "noble" thing by confessing to Atan's father how he had been coerced into the criminal act.

After the newlyweds returned from their honeymoon, Atan and his father argued. His father disowned him but never reported the theft to the police. When his father died a couple of years later, Atan learned that he had transferred all of what he owned to the "honest" accomplice. Atan was left with nothing but the old car in which he fled when his father threatened to call the police. Atan, thereafter, became a bitter and vengeful man.

By then the honeymoon was over, and Rojiah realised that Atan was nothing more than a lecher preying on stupid, lonesome women such as she. Soon, all her first husband's inheritance was exhausted. She at last had to work as a maid for a wealthy family some ten kilometres away from her home to earn a living for her family. She did not stay in. Atan would send her to work early in the morning and fetch her later in the evening. By the time she reached home, she would be too tired for anything but sleep. Atan, on the other hand, made little effort to secure a job.

After Rojiah started working, Atan, deprived of wifely attention, had spent most of his time in a sleazy pool parlour, where he befriended a waitress. She never revealed her age, but from her looks alone she could easily have been ten years older than him. Still, she listened as he described the woes of a husband whose wife cared more for her work than him. The waitress, herself a widow of several years after her husband had been killed in a road accident, also provided more intimate services for the right price, not that she could charge any premium at her age.

Atan had quite a talent for pool, and thus, apart from the monthly allowance from his wife, his daily bread was supplemented by winnings from pool games against poor souls who were either newcomers to the place or regulars who were cajoled into playing (and losing) a game with him.

Atan became one of the waitress's regular patrons. Some nights, after dropping off Rojiah back home, he would go out again to haunt the pool parlour and to meet the waitress. When her shift was over, they would use the makeshift bedroom in the back of the pool parlour for their tryst.

Then one day, Rojiah's employers' eldest daughter was getting married, and they planned for a huge reception. They requested for her to stay on for the night to help with the preparation and the following night to help with the cleaning up. She was reluctant, but on the premise of extra pay and a day off after the reception, she agreed. This she told Atan when he came in the evening to fetch her, and Atan only cursed her and suggested that she just stay there and never come home. He left her standing by the roadside, crying silently.

Of course, Atan did not go back home. Instead, he went to the pool parlour, played a few rounds, and attempted to drown his frustration and anger with two bottles of beer. Then he realised he didn't have any money. The owner, with the help of two well-built men, took his watch and threw him out the back door into the alley. The sympathetic waitress cursed the owner, who, in turn, told her not to come for work tomorrow.

The old waitress rushed outside to Atan's aid. She helped him to his car, and they both went back to Atan's house.

At home, Sue had fallen asleep on the wooden floor in the living room while listening to the radio and reading an entertainment magazine her mother sometimes brought back from work. She was awakened by the sound of someone fumbling to unlock the front door. Sue looked at the old wind-up clock with its swinging pendulum and was surprised to see that it was already eleven. Her mother should have been home a few hours ago with her stepfather. She was a bit wary of whoever the person on the other side of the door could be, although she was expecting to see her stepfather and her mother. Sue was used to being alone in the house. Since her mother had started working, she had been left to her own devices most of the time. She preferred it that way, being left to do whatever she pleased, whenever she felt like it.

As the door opened, Sue froze for a few moments when she could not recognise the person standing over the threshold. Then she saw her stepfather behind the stranger. The stranger smiled at her. She did not respond.

"Hello," the stranger greeted her.

Sue kept quiet.

"Hey, Sudarseh, go to sleep. Tomorrow is a school day. Why are you still up?" Her father looked angry.

"Where's my mother?" Sue asked.

"She's has to work late. Go inside now!" Atan's voice was rising.

"Who is this?" Sue asked.

"My friend. Go to your room, or I'll give you the cane … now!"

Sue picked up her magazines and her little security pillow and ran into her bedroom.

"Don't you come out of there!" Atan shouted after her.

Sue did not intend to. She felt sad and missed her mother. She prayed that her mother was all right and that she would come home soon. She fell asleep with her head buried under her pillow to block out the sounds from her stepfather's room, which was next to hers.

She did not know how long she was asleep. At first she thought she was dreaming. There was a commotion coming from her stepfather's room. She thought she heard a scream.

Then she heard someone running on the wooden floor of the stilted house, heading out the door. She went to her bedroom door, opened a small slit, and peeked outside. She saw the strange woman desperately trying to unlock the front door. She was half naked, with one hand propping a crumpled sheet against her body and the other trying to unlatch the wooden door. It wouldn't budge. Then she turned around, realising someone was behind her. The next thing Sue saw was her mother's back and a knife in her right hand. Rojiah approached the woman, who now had her back against the door and was asking for forgiveness.

"I'm sorry, I'm sorry," she repeated over and over again.

Rojiah stopped a few inches from her, raised the knife above her head, and brought it down several times on the woman.

Sue rushed out and hugged her mother from behind.

"Mother! No! Stop it! Stop it!" Sue shouted. And her mother did. She turned around, released the bloody knife, and got down to her knees, hugging Sue as tightly as she could. Over her mother's shoulder, Sue saw the streaks of blood on the door and the pooling blood collecting under the limp body of her stepfather's "friend." Then she wondered about Atan.

"Mother, where's Uncle Atan?" Sue never could bring herself to call Atan a fatherly name.

Sue felt her mother's body shake as she began to cry.

"Please forgive me, Sue. Please forgive me," she whispered in Sue's ear. She relaxed her hold on Sue, smiled, and kissed Sue's forehead. She picked up the knife and asked again for Sue's forgiveness. Then she extended her arms away from her body, pointed the knife at herself, and plunged the knife into her belly.

Sue screamed, "Mother! No!" but her mother was already doubled over and falling sideways. Sue did not know what to do. She just stood there watching her mother crumple down into a heap on the wooden floor.

Just then, Sue heard a moan from behind her. Looking around, Sue saw her stepfather staggering out of the bedroom holding his stomach with one bloody hand and steadying himself on the door frame with the other.

"Go to the Penghulus house. Get help," Atan said in a whisper.

Sue froze.

"Get help! Sue, go the Penghulu house now! Help me!" Atan started screaming.

Sue snapped out of her stupor and was about to run out the front door, but the woman's body was lying against it. Sue ran to the kitchen, unlatched the back door, and ran out into the night.

*****

Rojiah had asked her employer if she could be excused after the preparations were done. By that time it was already almost two in the morning. Her employers' driver had agreed to send Rojiah home in his own car after she told him how distressed she was by her husband's response to the prospect of her staying the night. Her employer agreed to let her go but made her promise she would be back by seven the next morning.

When she reached home, it was all dark and quiet, and she sneaked in as quietly as possible so as not to wake up Sue and Atan. She first looked in on Sue, who was sleeping soundly. Then she tried to open her bedroom door and was surprised that it was locked. From the slits between the door leaves, she saw light from within. Then she heard voices, a man's and a woman's. She peered through the slit and saw the back of her husband and the hands of a woman caressing it.

At first she felt regret and remorse, blaming herself for abandoning her husband. She walked softly over to Sue's room, intending to lie down next to the only thing in this world that mattered to her: her one and only offspring, Sudarseh. Then, looking at the sleeping Sue, she realised that she had been the one making all the sacrifices. She was reminded of her first husband, who had worked hard to provide for her and Sue. And she had killed him. She remembered the day when she told her husband, as he came through the door after a long trip to Singapore, that she wanted a divorce. She told him she had found someone who loved her and gave her all the attention she wanted. In anger, her husband walked right out of the house again and drove away. He never came back. The police came the next day to tell Rojiah that her husband had died after his car collided head-on with a timber lorry.

Rojiah had felt genuinely sad and cried when she heard the news, but Atan moved quickly into her life, knowing how much she would be inheriting. Rojiah's husband's carpet business was not exactly flourishing, but he had taken an insurance on his own life, and Rojiah told Atan that it was worth at least a hundred thousand ringgit.

Now, as she stood looking at her sleeping daughter, anger flushed over her. Atan fooled her. Atan took advantage of her. Now the luxurious life provided by her first husband was gone. She had taken the trouble to find a job to put food on the table, and Atan had brought back to her house a prostitute.

She walked out of Sue's room, went to the kitchen, and took the big knife from the kitchen cabinet drawer. Then she went back to her bedroom and knocked on the door.

"Don't disturb, Sue!" Atan shouted from within.

Rojiah knocked on the door again, this time with the hilt of the knife.

"Don't disturb, Sue. Don't you understand?" Atan shouted again.

Rojiah could hear the woman saying something. Then, just as Rojiah was about to knock on the door again, she heard it being unlatched. She tightened her grip on the hilt of the knife. The moment the door opened, Rojiah lifted her hand with the knife, sticking it into Atan's pot belly. Atan just looked at the place where Rojiah had stabbed him and then back at Rojiah. She pulled the knife out and stuck it into him again. He fell backwards on his buttocks. Then he curled onto his left side in a foetal position and stayed there, motionless.

The women, gathering the bed sheet to cover herself, screamed. Rojiah came for her. The woman scrambled over to the other side of the bed and crouched down, screaming, "Help! Help!"

Rojiah came around the bed after her. The woman slithered under the bed and came out the other side. She ran out of the room, stepping over Atan, to the front door. She fumbled with the latches of the front door, her hands shaking with fear. The latches would not budge. She could feel the vibration of Rojiah's footsteps on the wooden floor. She turned around to face Rojiah and begged for her forgiveness. Then the knife came down upon her repeatedly, until she lost consciousness.

*****

Sue came back to the house, with the Penghulu and two villagers in tow. One of the villagers fainted when he saw the bloody scene. The Penghulu thought everyone was dead, but then he heard Atan moaning. The one villager still standing was instructed by the Penghulu to get to the nearest public telephone and call for the police and a few ambulances.

The woman was dead by the time the ambulances and the police came, but Rojiah had failed to kill Atan, and neither was she successful in killing herself. Both Atan and Rojiah were warded for a few days at the General Hospital after being duly stitched up. No vital internal organs were damaged, but the incident had rendered Atan impotent.

Rojiah, however, was transferred to the psychiatric ward after a nurse found her in the women's toilet, attempting to cut her wrist with a pair of scissors she had stolen from the nurse station. Thereafter, she regressed quickly into a manic depressive state, with suicidal tendencies, and thus the police considered the case closed.

Now the once-beautiful Rojiah lived in a home for the mentally ill managed by the state welfare department. Sue would visit whenever she could. Rojiah had lost her memory and her mind. Most of the time she sat in one corner and stared into nothingness, crying.

After the bloody incident, Atan and Sue both agreed they could not stay at the same house, and so they moved away to settle down in a new village on the fringe of Muar town. It was not all that far away from their original village, since Sue wanted to be near her mother's home. In the new village, with new neighbours, their bloody history was kept secret, although after a while there were rumours fluttering among the village folk that Sue's mother was a madwoman.

Atan still could not hold a job for long. Sue, after she finished her SPM exams, knowing full well she would fail them, went on to find a job to sustain the both of them.

*****

That was almost two decades ago. Sue got out of bed and changed into a sarong and an old T-shirt. In the mirror of her small dresser, she saw her swollen eyes and a small cut above her left eyebrow, where she had hit her head on the bed when she fell in her attempt to escape the enraged Atan. Atan was really angry. He had actually whipped her with his belt. Perhaps it was more shameful than painful for a thirty-one-year-old woman to be whipped by her stepfather. For most of her life, her stepfather had never really cared for her, but each time someone showed interest in her, he became overprotective. She knew that Atan knew he couldn't live without her. She was and would always be the breadwinner of this household, and Atan was really protecting himself.

She thought about Rocky. She didn't know if he really loved her. She suspected that he was already married, but for Muslims, polygamy was not illegal. Rocky was her chance of escaping to start a new life. And Rocky was the only one in a long time bold enough to disregard Atan's reputation as an ill-tempered and vulgar man who overly cared for his only stepdaughter. Or perhaps Rocky was ignorant.

What worried her most was that Atan came back too soon after he and Rocky were supposed to be duelling at the old cemetery. She was afraid for Rocky. Something was not right, and intuitively she knew that she had probably seen the last of Rocky. She crumbled onto her bed and shook uncontrollably from utter sadness, suppressing a need to scream and shout.

"Oh Rocky, what have they done to you?" she whispered.

She would have looked for him, but her stepfather had locked her bedroom door from the outside.

*****

The manager was looking at some porn on the internet when Sue knocked on his office door. His immediate reaction was to exit from the website, but the site was still downloading some pictures, so he just turned the monitor off.

"Come in!" he shouted while adjusting himself.

Sue had come in earlier, after she clocked in, to see the manager. She told him that something must have happened to Rocky because she couldn't find him anywhere at the factory. He did not report for work, according to his immediate supervisor. His co-workers had no idea where he had gone, and even his house-mates said he never came home last night.

Now, a couple of hours later, Sue went to see the manager again. She was visibly distressed, and upon seeing her, the manager was visibly annoyed.

"Alamaaaak, is this about your Bangla boyfriend again? I told you already, Sue: I can't do anything. He's an illegal immigrant. If we report to the police, our boss sure will be jailed. Then we all would be out of work. Do you want that?" asked the manager.

"I know, Encik Hassan, I know. But can't we do something?" begged Sue.

"We? We? You mean you and me?" the manager sounded bemused.

"Er, we … the company, the other workers, his friends," said Sue.

"Friends? Hallo, Sue, when they come here, it's every man for himself. They all are immigrants. They just want to come here, make money, and then go back home. They don't want trouble, laa."

Sue stood there in the small office, looked at the floor, and cried silently.

"Sue, why laa you so shiok at the Bangla?" the manager said. His tone softened. "Why, no more Malay man here, is it? Look at me, I am available also what?"

"You? Encik Hassan, you are married, and you have six children already. What do mean available?" Sue sounded a little angered at the manager's insolence.

"Eyyy, I am a Muslim, laaa. I can have four," said the manager with a grin on his face and his hand stretched out towards Sue, showing her four grubby fingers.

Sue felt like spitting into his hand, but instead she turned around and walked out of the office. The manager shrugged and turned on the monitor again. His mouth opened slightly when he saw the fully downloaded image.

*****

That evening, after her shift ended, Sue decided to go to the police. *I don't care about the stupid factory or the stupid boss, or the stupid sex maniac manager. They don't care about me. Nobody does.*

The police were sympathetic, but she did not escape their chiding of "Aren't there any local guys?" with a head shake and a puff of disgust.

"So, you are saying that you suspect your stepfather may have done something to the Bangla?" the constable who took her statement said.

"I don't know. But he must've sent him somewhere or gotten someone to do something to Rocky," cried Sue.

"Rocky?"

"That's what we call him at the factory," explained Sue.

"So are you saying that he may have something to do with, err, Rocky's disappearance, but you are not sure? Why?"

"Because he came home too soon. After they went off to the old cemetery, he was home just a few minutes later. It's like he just left Rocky somewhere and came right home," Sue said, trying to hold herself together.

"Are sure about that?" asked the constable.

"Very sure," Sue said.

"Wait here, please." The constable suddenly looked grave. He left and then came back again with another, higher-ranking police officer.

"Cik Sudarseh? I am Inspector Chia. Thank you for making your statement. Actually, we found a body. One of your kampong folks confessed he killed a Bangla. We went looking for the body but couldn't find it where he said he left it. Then some schoolchildren found a body in a big drain by the side of the main road. We have his body at the hospital morgue. Do you think you can identify the body?"

Sue wasn't sure she wanted to do that, but she nodded her head.

It was Rocky. Sue was sure of it, even though the face was disfigured, his nose was visibly broken, his left cheek bone was exposed, and there were deep indentations on his neck. Sue broke down and vomited outside the morgue. Chia had given her a plastic bag, and she filled it between her sobs.

"I'm sorry, Cik Sudarseh." Chia was sympathetic.

"How did he die?" Sue asked, after she had collected herself and thrown the plastic bag in a nearby dustbin.

"We are not sure. The coroner said there was water in his lungs, so most likely the real cause of death was drowning. But his body ... well, you saw it. Somebody tried to strangle him. And there were blows to his face, probably with a shovel or something,"

"I think I need to go to the washroom," replied Sue.

*****

"Where have you been? I am hungry," asked Atan almost the moment Sue stepped over the threshold of their house. He was lying on the sofa looking annoyed.

"Nowhere," answered Sue without breaking her stride. She disappeared behind the curtain that hung in the doorway of her bedroom.

"Wah! Testing your power with me, hah?" Atan said with a cynical grin on his face.

"She was at the police station, Encik Atan," a voice said from the front door. Inspector Chia was standing in the doorway. "And I think you have to follow me to the police station."

Immediately, Atan bolted to the kitchen. Chia didn't move. Atan bumped into a constable waiting for him at the back exit.

*****

Justice, Sue felt as she rose from the bench in the courtroom, was done, at last. Her stepfather was found guilty of accessory to murder while two others, one a self-proclaimed shaman and the other the village idiot, were convicted for attempted murder. According to Chia, the village idiot, named Udin, confessed to hitting Rocky unconscious with a shovel before the shaman tried to strangle him to death. All of them would be put away for a long time.

But rather than relieved, she felt sad and lonely. She had nobody. Her boyfriend was dead, her mother was committed to an asylum, and now her stepfather was jailed.

Turning around, her sadness deepened when she saw how empty the courtroom was. She sighed and walked out into the midmorning sun. Outside, she saw Inspector Chia having a smoke with two other policemen. He gave her a smile and a thumbs-up. She smiled wryly back.

She didn't know where to go. She had taken leave for the day, thinking the sentencing would take a long time. Now she had the whole day to herself. Maybe she should go shopping or go visit her mother. Or maybe she would just take a walk around town. It was such a lovely day.

She looked at her watch and hailed a taxi. She told the driver to go to the factory. She would make it there before the afternoon shift started, but she would have to see the manager to cancel her leave. She hated meeting the manager.

Baked Macaroni

"What are you waiting for, Cikgu?" asked Ramli.

"Who," said Aliana.

"You," said Ramli.

"I mean, I'm waiting for a 'who', not a 'what'," Aliana elaborated, hoping that Ramli would not carry the conversation further.

"OK, who are you waiting for?"

"Nobody. I am waiting for the taxi which I charter every day to take me home," said Aliana. There was exasperation in her voice, which she did little to hide.

"Then my original question was right. You are waiting for a 'what', not a 'who'." Ramli smiled.

Aliana smiled and looked down the road. It was deserted.

"I am waiting for my daughter," Ramli said. He felt nervous talking to Aliana, and he hoped it wasn't obvious. But he was determined not to let this chance pass. Ramli saw her many times before, waiting for her taxi here, at this bus stop almost every school day. He thought she was beautiful. She was tall and slender and her hijab-framed, fair face has soft, lovely features.

"I know," Aliana responded with a smile.

"She's having some kind of briefing on the upcoming exams," Ramli added.

"I know," Aliana responded again. *Where is that taxi?* She took out her hand phone and dialled the taxi company number.

"I think she's doing OK. I think she'll get five As. She's very hard-working."

Aliana started to say 'I know' again but stopped herself. Instead she just smiled. She had her phone clasped to her right ear.

"Hallo, Cikgu. Sorry, I am on the way, just now got bad jam. Five minutes, I'll be there." The line was disconnected. Aliana thought the taxi driver must have fallen asleep again, like the last time. The last time his wife answered the phone and told Aliana he was asleep.

"Cikgu, why don't you buy a car? I see you wait for the taxi every day. Sometimes I see you are still here when everybody else has gone," said Ramli.

You should be too, thought Aliana. "I don't have a driving license" instead came out of her mouth. It was a lie.

"Oh, why don't you get one? I think it's quite easy nowadays," Ramli continued, seemingly oblivious of the irritation he was causing.

"I don't have time." *Where is that taxi?* Aliana thought as she peered down the road.

"Good afternoon, Cikgu!" Syafiqa said, almost startling Aliana. "Your taxi is late again, huh?"

"Good afternoon, Syafiqa. Yes, he's late again. How was the briefing?" asked Aliana, a little relieved that Syafiqa had arrived, which meant that she and her father would soon leave.

"OK, I guess." Syafiqa shrugged. She hadn't paid much attention at the briefing. Syafiqa stood between Ramli and Aliana for a while and then realised that her father was not getting up.

"What are you waiting for, Abah?" asked Syafiqa.

"Er, I just want to make sure Cikgu Aliana gets her taxi. This place is deserted," Ramli said, smiling at Aliana.

"OK." Syafiqa looked puzzled. She sat down on the cool cement bus stop seat.

"Abah, why don't we send Cikgu home?" Syafiqa asked Ramli after a while.

"Yes, Cikgu, we can send you home. Where do you live?" Ramli asked Aliana.

"It's OK. I don't want to trouble you. Besides, my taxi is coming soon," Aliana declined the offer. But then her telephone rang. When she answered it, she could hear the sound of heavy traffic in the background.

"Cikgu, very sorry. I was rushing to fetch you, but now I've hit somebody's rear end. It's very bad, and my car has to be towed." The taxi driver sounded breathless. "Sorry, ah … Can you call another taxi, ah?"

"What choice do I have?" Aliana said and disconnected the line. Then she dialled the radio taxi number. It rang for a long time, and Aliana almost gave up.

"Hello, Blue Colour Radio taxi. How can I help you?" said a voice at last.

"Yes, can you send a taxi to Sekolah Kebangsaan Bandaraya? Yes, yes … one hour? Why so long? OK la, OK la … I wait at the bus stop." Aliana disconnected the line and sighed.

"Where do you live? I'll send you. If you are not comfortable, you can call your husband to ask his permission," Ramli said, guessing accurately Aliana's plight.

"Cikgu Aliana is not married la Abah," Syafiqa said.

"Oh, then come, we'll send you home. No trouble at all," Ramli said. He wondered if Aliana noted how pleased he was to know that Aliana was single.

"Come, Cikgu," Syafiqa said with a great smile. She liked Aliana, the English teacher.

"Yes, Cikgu. You can sit in the back if you are not comfortable," Ramli said, giving a reassuring smile to Aliana.

"It's OK. I've got another taxi," Aliana said with a tinge of doubt in her voice.

It was already two in the afternoon. And once the few remaining year six teachers and students were gone, the school would be empty. The bus stop was practically deserted except for Aliana, Ramli, and Syafiqa.

Aliana suddenly realised that the school was perched atop a hill. She could see the road stretching to the right and left of her all the way down to the junction with traffic lights at both ends of the road. She could see traffic moving across the range of sight at both ends of the road, but none of the vehicles turned in to the road coming towards her. She could see the heat rising from the hot asphalt.

It was getting really awkward, with the three of them sitting there in silence. Aliana wished Ramli would just go home. She tried to sneak a look at Ramli just to see what he was doing. She pretended to look for her taxi, as if it might be coming from the other end of the road, but their eyes met.

"It's OK, really. This is a good neighbourhood. Zero crime rate." Aliana smiled at Ramli. "And I'm sure you have to get back to work, right?"

Ramli thought, *she has a lovely smile.* "I'm not working," he replied.

"Unemployed? Oh, I'm sorry. How about your wife, is she working?" Aliana sounded genuinely concerned. *The economy is really bad,* she concluded.

"Mama passed away three years ago. She had cancer," Syafiqa said in a matter-of-fact way.

Aliana was shocked, more by the way Syafiqa said it rather than the information.

"Oh, I'm sorry, my dear. I didn't know," Aliana said, reaching out and rubbing Syafiqa's back as she sat between her and Ramli.

"It's OK. Abah said she's in a good place. Her grave is spacious and full of light. And she sleeps soundly and painlessly until judgement day, and I pray for her every day," Syafiqa said to Aliana, rubbing her teacher's back in return as if comforting her. "I know she is in a better place than this. This life was full of pain for her." Her voice trailed off a little at the end. Syafiqa leaned her head on Aliana's breast.

"Of course she is," Aliana said, hoping Ramli did not notice the little crack in her voice. She put a fist to her mouth as if suppressing a cough and cleared her throat. But really she wanted to make sure that no liquid flowed out of her nostrils.

"Why don't you let us send you home, Cikgu? No ulterior motives, I guarantee. You can call the police. Here's my IC," Ramli said. The heat was getting to be unbearable.

Aliana gave a little laugh. "I'm sure the taxi will be here soon," she said.

"OK, then we wait until it comes," Ramli said. They all went quiet again.

"Aren't you hungry, Fiqa?" asked Aliana, thinking that if Syafiqa said yes, it would compel Ramli to go home. But then she realised she herself felt hungry. She had eaten some fried noodles during recess, but that was all. She had skipped breakfast this morning. The taxi driver was too early and was already waiting for her at six. She hated it when somebody was waiting for her. She felt pressured. That was the real reason she didn't drive. She used to, but all the other drivers were so impatient and ungrateful.

"No, Abah made some baked macaroni. I ate some just now. There's some more. Do you want some?" Syafiqa unzipped her backpack and took out a plastic container. "Here." She held out the container to Aliana.

Aliana didn't want any, although she was impressed that that Ramli could cook. But she did not want to disappoint

Syafiqa, who was already holding out the container to her. Anyway, she was a little hungry, and she was curious about how Ramli's baked macaroni tasted.

Aliana opened the container, and a lovely smell of meat and herbs and cheese made her mouth water. She took one piece of macaroni gingerly with the tip of her forefinger and thumb and popped it into her mouth. She almost closed her eyes, expecting a terrible taste. But it was delicious.

"Hmmm, that's really delicious. You are a good cook," Aliana said to Ramli.

"Of course, Cikgu. If not, who will come to our restaurant?" Syafiqa said. "Cikgu, you finish it. I can't eat any more. Abah always gives big portions. I don't want to be fat."

Aliana thought how ungainly it was for an unmarried woman sitting by herself at a bus stop to accept food offerings from a little girl cooked by her father.

"You don't mind?" Aliana asked Syafiqa, moving her gaze to Ramli.

"You finish it, please, Cikgu. It will all go to waste. I don't have any brothers or sister or pets to give it to," Syafiqa said, which, Aliana thought, sounded like a hint to Ramli.

Does she want a pet or siblings? Aliana wondered. "Thank you," Aliana said when she saw Ramli give a little nod and smile, as if he knew the unease she was feeling.

"You can use this fork. I washed it. Abah always asks me to wash it before putting it back in my bag to take home," Syafiqa said.

"So you have a restaurant, Encik ... er ..." Aliana peeked at Syafiqa's name tag. "Err ... Ramli?"

"Just a small coffee shop," Ramli said humbly.

"It's called Chez Jasmine, after Mama," Syafiqa said.

Aliana thought Syafiqa looked sad when she said that. For some reason, she felt guilty about eating the baked macaroni.

"I thought you said it's delicious," Ramli said when he saw Aliana seemed to have stopped eating and was just staring at his macaroni. "It's OK, Cikgu," Ramli said as if reading Aliana's mind. "You flatter me if you finish it."

"Thank you. I am a little hungrier than I thought," Aliana said. She started poking at the macaroni with the fork Syafiqa had given her. "Chez Jasmine. I've heard of it. It's in Sri Hartamas, isn't it?" Aliana said, pointing in the general direction where she thought Sri Hartamas was with the fork.

"Yes," Ramli replied. "Have you been there? I don't think so,"

"Why don't you think so?"

"Because if you have, I would have noticed you." Ramli smiled.

Aliana blushed. Ramli sounded sincere, but she knew she had walked into that corny pick-up line. Ramli thought Aliana looked sweet when she blushed, and he couldn't help staring at her. Aliana thought there was something on her face.

"Is there something on my face?" Aliana asked Syafiqa, almost whispering. Syafiqa was reading a little ghost story book. On the cover there was a picture of a boy trapped between the jaws of a giant Venus flytrap.

Syafiqa squinted at Aliana's face and shook her head. "Cikgu, I'm bored. Won't you please let Abah send you home? Please, please," pleaded Syafiqa.

"Why don't you go home? I'll be OK. They've sent me another taxi,"

"That was almost an hour ago, Cikgu. I don't want to leave you here alone too. Please come and let Abah send you home." Syafiqa made one of her cute faces with a mock frown.

Aliana sighed. "OK, because you asked." Aliana put the cover back on the now empty plastic container and washed the fork with some water from a tumbler in her bag. She looked away from Ramli and took a swig of drink from the same container. She gathered her umbrella, which was leaning against the cement seat.

Ramli stood up and stretched. He felt he had been sitting a long time. "You guys wait here. I'll bring the car," he said, walking away.

*****

"So you are self-employed," said Aliana while waiting for the light to change at the junction at the end of the school road. She was sitting in the passenger seat of Ramli's car.

"Huh?" Ramli seemed to be in another place, staring blankly at the red light with a little smile on his face.

"You said you are unemployed. But actually you are self-employed, your own boss," Aliana said a little louder, over the music playing from the radio.

"I said I'm not working. You said I was unemployed," Ramli said with a grin on his face.

"But that's not true either. You are working … for yourself."

"Someone said that it's not working when you do the thing you like," Ramli said as they joined the main flow of traffic.

"Abah, is Cikgu Aliana going to be my new mama?" asked Syafiqa.

Ramli blushed. "Please don't embarrass me, Fiqa," he said, looking at Syafiqa in the rear-view mirror. "Sorry, Cikgu," he continued.

Syafiqa poked her head in between the two front seats and looked at Ramli and then to Aliana.

"Actually, I just realised, Abah, this is the first time I'm riding in the backseat since Mama passed away. And Cikgu, you're the first lady ever to ride in our car since then," Syafiqa observed.

"Is that true?" asked Aliana. She seemed to be more attracted to Ramli.

"Now that Fiqa mentioned it, yes. I never really thought about it," Ramli answered.

"What were you waiting for?" asked Aliana.

"Who," said Ramli.

"You," said Aliana.

"No, I mean, I'm not waiting for a 'what' but a 'who'." Ramli grinned.

"OK, who are you waiting for?" Aliana gave a little laugh.

Ramli took his time to answer. He had never been one to tell of his inner thoughts and feelings. But with Aliana it felt different. "I don't know," he found himself saying. "Losing someone you love hurts. And I am really worried about Fiqa. I just wanted to make sure she's OK, you know. So I just sort of kept myself busy with the restaurant and taking care of Fiqa. It does cross my mind to remarry. God knows I get pressure from people around me. But I just can't bring myself to, er … substitute Jasmine. I feel like I would be cheating on her, if I were to start seeing other women. But then, Fiqa is getting older. She'll need a motherly figure to talk about ... you know, women stuff. If you know what I mean."

Aliana did not reply. *I, more than anyone else, know about the pain of heartbreak, having to lose someone you love,* she thought to herself, looking down at her hands. She wanted to let her heart out to Ramli too. But she decided against it. He didn't need to know about her lost love.

*****

Aliana binti Hasbullah had always wanted to be a teacher. Her father, Hasbullah bin Hashim, was a teacher, a renowned and highly respected figure in Muar. Cikgu Sebol, as he was known, was the headmaster of the local high school who went on to become the head of the state education department, the position he held until the time he retired.

But it was her mother's tenacity and perseverance that motivated and inspired her to be a teacher. Aliana's mother was often referred to as Cikgu Maryam, though she never had a formal education. Aliana's mother taught herself to read and write, and later taught other women the same, at a time when literate women were a rarity.

Her father passed away almost ten years ago; her mother lived with her sister in her hometown. She was ninety-one years old and wheelchair bound, yet she had a mind as sharp as anyone half her age.

Aliana's first and only love was a boy who was her classmate at a night tuition class for form-five students (seventeen-year-olds) organised by some young graduates who couldn't find a job. He was shy but always managed to get a seat directly behind Aliana in class. In the day, Aliana went to an all-girls school while he went to a co-ed school with a rather notorious reputation.

His name was Razali, or Zali for short. His friends called him Wak, due to his Javanese origins and because at home his family spoke to each other in Javanese dialect.

Throughout the year, they were very much aware of each other. Stolen glances, little smiles every time they passed each other, and the insistence of Zali to sit as close as he could to her sent out mutually understood secret messages that they liked each other. Other students notice this and teased them, but both their parents had warned that they should not be having any kind of boy-girl relationships until they had secured a college admission, at the very least.

Aliana was accepted into one of the most highly reputable teachers colleges up north, in Pulau Pinang; while Zali was offered a degree in electrical engineering course down south in Johor Bahru.

At the night tuition farewell party, realising he might not see her again, Zali mustered up the courage to approach Aliana. He asked if they could stay in touch with each other and said that he liked her very much.

Secretly, Aliana gave a sigh of relief after she had given him the assurance that she would write to him, in a letter addressed to his home, to inform him of her college address once she was settled in. Zali said he would ask his older brother to forward any letters for him to his college in Johor Bahru. Thereafter, all communications would be via letters addressed directly to their respective colleges.

It remained a long-distance love affair. The only time they actually met was during Eid Fitri, when the group of ex-night tuition classmates would gather and visit each other's houses, as was the tradition during this festivity.

She kept a picture of him; he kept one of her. He kept it pressed between the pages of one of his textbooks and looked at it during boring lectures, before he went to sleep, and each time he was replying her letters.

Aliana did well in her studies. She was in the dean's list for every semester. She loved everything about her college. She loved learning, she liked her friends and her lecturers, and they loved her in return. She had a bouncy, optimistic personality, so she was always in the fray of almost every party and get-together.

Zali's college life was exactly the opposite. He could not cope with his studies. He did not like the Maths lecturer, he could not understand the Filipino slang of the Physics lecturer, and he loathed the English class–compulsory for all students–because they laughed at him when he tried to speak English in his thick Javanese accent. He managed to scrape through the first year but had to repeat the third semester, failed, and was expelled.

He was ashamed. His parents had never expected him to be an over-achiever, but he had always been at the higher end of the mediocrity spectrum. This expectation and his own pride and self-respect prevented him from telling his parents of his predicament, as he struggled during his studies. But now that he was expelled, he had to tell the truth. His father was furious, but his mother was sympathetic. His father stopped speaking to him for a few days, but eventually his parents asked him what he planned to do next. Zali said he would still like to get some sort of paper qualification, but since it was unlikely he would get a scholarship – he even had to repay the government for the scholarship he had received for the two years he was in college – he would like to go to Kuala Lumpur to find a job and go to night classes to get a diploma, perhaps in computer programming. His parents agreed.

A month later, in Kuala Lumpur, Zali stayed with his sister and her family – her banker husband and their two little boys, aged five and three – in a suburban area on the outskirts of the city. He commuted daily to the bank, where he worked as a cheque-clearing clerk. After work, he would take a bus to a private college, where he learned about computers and computer programming. All this while, he never replied any of Aliana's letters.

She only learned of his expulsion when she forced herself to call Zali's house. Luckily, Zali's elder brother answered the phone. She was bracing herself for a barrage of questions should Zali's father picked up the phone. Zali's brother was sympathetic. He apologised on behalf of Zali and told her that he had left for Kuala Lumpur about a month ago and now worked in a bank. Aliana asked for his address, and Zali's brother complied.

Finally, after another month or so and three letters asking the same questions, Aliana found a letter on her dormitory bed. Her friend had gone to the college administration office and picked up all the letters for her dorm-mates.

Peace be upon you, Aliana.

I pray to Allah that this letter finds you in the best of health. I must first apologise for my long silence. I am sure you know by now what has happened to me. I failed. I failed my family, and to a certain extent, I feel I failed you too.

In our letters to each other, we have on several occasions touched on our plans for the future – our future together as husband and wife, as parents, and eventually to have our own family.

As a man, one who were brought up on traditional values and is expected to perpetuate these values down to our succeeding generations, I will always want to be the provider. Unfortunately, my failure to secure a college degree now means that I have wasted about two years of my life. Now it means that I have to start all over again.

This is shameful for me.

How can I be worthy of the hand in marriage of an educated woman such as you? Can I impose upon you to wait for me to restart my education, when there are many more men, better educated than me, more worthy to be your husband?

If Allah has fated that we are to be together, no matter how far and how long we will be apart, we will find each other. But for now, I ask that we go our separate ways so that both of us can concentrate on our now-separate lives. I think it is better this way.

I pray for your success, that one day there will be students who will call you Cikgu Aliana, a title, unlike many other job titles, which will be permanently attached on those chosen ones who have a hand in the success of every world leader.

I will always love you.

Yours truly,
Razali bin Sariman

Aliana read the letter again. She did not understand the contents. *Traditional values? More worthy men? He thinks it's better this way? He thinks? Why can't we discuss this first? Does he think that I befriended him because he was going to be an engineer? Does he think that my love for him has a price?*

She was angry. Se crumpled up the letter and threw it into the dustbin. Then she realised her friends were watching. She broke down, and her dorm-mates came around to pacify her.

*****

"Am I going the right way?" Ramli asked.

Aliana inhaled sharply in horror as she looked out the window. "Oh no, we missed the turn. Oh, I'm so sorry. Now you'll have to go all the way to end of this expressway to make a U–turn – and pay a toll." Aliana was pinching her lower lip, regretting the bother she had caused Ramli.

"That's a long way," Ramli said seriously.

"This can mean only one thing," Ramli continued, pretending to look annoyed. "You'll have to come with us to our restaurant," he said, this time with a grin on his face.

"Your restaurant?"

"Actually, I have to get some of the stuff in the boot back to the restaurant," Ramli said. "Do you mind? Or do you have some other plans?"

"Hmm, I planned to take a nap," Aliana said jokingly.

"I would like you to see my restaurant," Ramli said.

"OK, I think I'd like to see your restaurant."

Ramli flicked the indicator light on and turned at the next exit.

****

Zali slowed down to a halt in front of the bus stop. There wasn't anybody there. He sighed and reached for the radio.

"Hallo! I am at the school, nobody here laa. I think the passenger left already," he said to the woman on the other end of the line.

"OK loh," the woman said. And she just went quiet.

"No other calls?" Zali asked.

"Err … No la," the woman said.

"OK." Zali sighed. He put the receiver down and sat in his taxi, deciding what to do next. The place was deserted. He rolled down his window and felt heat of the late afternoon on his face. Looking at the school, he thought about a girl he had once known a long time ago. She was probably a teacher now – a very good one, the kind of teacher that the pupils loved. He rolled the window back up and lowered the volume of the two-way radio. He reached for the lever at the side of his seat, leaned back, put his right arm over his eyes, and tried to sleep. How he wished he had studied harder in college, or at least finished the computer programming course. Maybe he shouldn't have taken up the offer from that syndicate that altered cheques, gotten caught, and spent time in jail.

The Last Pontianak

A Ghost's Story

A Pontianak is a ghost from Malay and Indonesian folklore. They are said to be the spirits of women who died while pregnant or while giving birth. They transform themselves into beautiful women to lure men before killing them for blood (and some say for their genitals). However, legend has it that if a man can embed a nail in the back of the neck of a Pontianak, she will be permanently transformed into her beautiful self for as long as the nail is not removed.

Once there was a tall tree in the forest. It was so tall that when I sat in it, I could not see the base. When I looked down, all I could see was more foliage. I loved sitting up there. The lowest of the branches were almost at the same level as the road that was built by humans on the side of a hill, not far away. I would sit on my favourite branch and hum songs from long ago, though I couldn't recall the names of the songs, any of the words, or where I heard them from. I liked watching the humans pass by on the road in their carriages.

I could not recall the first time I sat in this lovely tree, but I did remember a time when there was no road. When there were only trees in every direction, for as far as the eye can see … Not that I could see much, since I only came out at night.

I was a Pontianak. That was what I was told by the midget ghost everybody calls Toyol. He's a thief, that Toyol. He said he used to have a human master who fed him blood. He had to suck the blood from his master's big toe, which I thought was disgusting. Toyol said it was nice and he only wished his master had taken care of his feet a bit more, perhaps wearing socks more often. Unfortunately, one night, his master died. He tried to suck blood from another human's toe, but the human started screaming and woke the whole village up.

The next thing he knew, he was sent here in this forest by a shaman. He's off blood now, he said. Now he only eats fruit. Some humans planted an orchard full of mangoes, bananas, papayas, and pineapples some distance from our area. Toyol would steal some of these fruits and bring them into his lair, which was a big hole in a dead tree trunk. Sometime we would both sit in the tree and share a pineapple.

I was a female ghost. That was what the Djinn told me. The Djinn was the ghost in charge of this area. He was really big and muscular, with horns on his head, but rumours had it he too was abandoned by his human master. Nobody dared to ask him. He was really scary and seemed angry all the time. He was my protector, he told me. From what, I did not ask.

Then the humans came to build the road. At first a few of them came. They started to clear some land, built a house of some sort, and worked measuring the land from one end to another. The Djinn asked us to scare them off. We tried, but they just kept coming back. They brought more humans, who came and screamed out loud to let them be because they meant no harm. The screaming annoyed the Djinn. He possessed one of the workers and spoke to the humans to get out or bear the consequences. But the humans were relentless. They called in more of the same kind of screaming humans, this time in many different languages. And they burned stinking incense, which gave me a terrible headache and made me vomit blood. We gave up and stopped scaring them. I personally think, in hindsight, that was a good decision.

The humans built their road, and in all honesty, I don't know what the Djinn was so riled up about. Maybe we lost a lot of trees, but when the road was completed and the humans started to use it in their carriages, we had more humans to scare.

And talking about scaring humans – that part of my existence I did not understand. Why did we have to scare these humans? I asked Toyol, but he said that's just the way it is. Toyol was the only one I could consult with. The other ghosts were Pocongs. They were all wrapped up in white, with only their faces exposed. Their eyes were always shut, and they didn't talk. They just jumped about aimlessly in the forest.

Up in my tree, singing my nameless tune, I spent the nights looking out onto the road. Some nights there were a lot of those human carriages in many forms and sizes, traversing the road. I loved watching them. It was like a procession of lights. I would see those going away in red and those coming were in yellow. But these processions did not happen often. On most nights, there would be a lot of the carriages in the early evening and then fewer and fewer deeper into the night. Past midnight, the road would be almost deserted save for one or two lonely travellers speeding by.

Once in a while we would accidentally kill these humans. I didn't know if we were supposed to. Toyol said that the villagers accused him of killing his master. He didn't know that humans needed to have blood in them to live, which made him think humans were really stupid. If his master needed blood in him, why did he let Toyol suck it out?

I killed one myself, I think. It was a nice moonlit night, and one of those lonely travellers in the hours past midnight stopped his carriage by the side of the road for some reason. Then a wonderful thing happened. Bright amber lights started to blink on all sides of the human carriage. I had never seen this before, and I wanted a closer look. So I flew to the road and approached the carriage. As I came near, the poor human stepped out of his carriage. He saw me, started screaming, clutched his chest, and fell to the ground, limp. I didn't know what to do, so I just left and flew back to my tree. I did not know what happened to the human. I hung around for a while, mesmerised by the blinking amber lights, but no other human carriages passed by. It was getting bright, and I was getting sleepy.

The Pocongs were the best at killing humans because there were a lot of them. Sometimes, as they jumped about here and there, one or two of them would end up on the road. The humans would try to avoid hitting them – I don't know why – and would swerve and lose control. Some ended up down at the bottom of the gorge, and some would crash their carriages into the retaining walls. Some survived, but most died on the spot. I think some of the dead humans turned into Pocongs. I'm not sure. But looking at those humans who died, their faces have the same expression as the Pocongs.

*****

The most disconcerting thing about being a ghost was that you could never really tell if the humans could see you. Some of them could, but some of them couldn't. I knew little baby humans could, because while I was in my tree, little baby humans in the human carriages sometimes waved at me. Some laughed when I make faces at them, and some cried.

Some bigger humans can see us, but most can't. I did not know the human I killed could see me.

Then it happened again. A human carriage – they call them cars – stopped by the roadside, at almost the same place the last one did, and it lit up just as the last one did. This time I waited a while for the human to appear from the carriage. I watched from my tree as a rather round human, without hair on his head, appeared from the belly of the carriage. His head was so shiny that for a moment I thought it was blinking, just like the carriage.

The human walked to the front of his carriage and opened the front portion of it. Then he went to the back and opened that part too. Then he stood there, looking around, waiting for something. (He later confessed that he was waiting for me.)

At that point, I was sure he was not one of those humans who could see me. So I thought that this would be a chance to take a closer look at those wonderful blinking lights, and I flew onto the road. When I reached near the carriage, the human was still standing at the back of his car. It looked like he was looking at me, but there was no expression on his face. I came closer, to a distance where most humans would flee or lose consciousness. But he just stood there, this small, round, bald human, and I was sure, though he was looking at me, he did not see me.

I floated past him, intending to go around the carriage to look at all the blinking lights. But the moment I passed the human, I felt a sharp pain at the back of my neck. I turned around immediately and only saw the human, standing there looking at me. The night seemed to turn bright with a blinding white light; my last thoughts were, *He saw me.*

*****

When I awoke, I was in a room. I was lying on something soft. It was very comfortable. The room was dark, but there were streaks of light from tiny holes on one side. I could hear people talking in low voices from within the darkness on the other side.

"Ahh, you are awake," said a voice. The human I had seen on the road appeared from the shadows, holding in his hand something with a small fire on top of it. This, I later learned, is a lamp, and the small fire was fuelled by the oil inside it. The fire frightened me, and I put my hand up to block the light out of my eyes.

"You can see me," I said.

"Yes, everybody can see you now. You've … err … changed," the human said with a smile. He looked around, walked to one side of the room, and came back.

I became more afraid when he suddenly thrust a mirror at me. In it, I saw the reflection of a human. I looked at my hands and realised that I had become one of them. My skin was no longer a pale white but pinkish.

Another figure appeared from the darkness, an old woman.

"You have changed, my child," she said. "But don't be afraid. We will take good care of you."

*****

Apparently, as a human, I was beautiful. I was married to the man in a small ceremony about a month or so after my transformation. My husband was very proud of having me as his wife. He and the old woman (who was his mother) had given me the name Seri.

My husband, whose name is Deman, conjured up a story of my origins. I was the daughter of a poor farmer who lived in a little-known village in the south of Siam. Deman told those who came to see his new beautiful wife that the poor farmer was so grateful for Deman's help that he insisted that Deman become his son-in-law, to become the son he never had. All this had happened only a few months ago, although what manner or form of help Deman provided was never divulged.

Despite the necessary lie – for no one would have believed the truth – Deman was a good and kind man. He doted on me and constantly asked if there was anything he could do to make me more comfortable.

Deman ran a food stall by the side of a road, much like the road I used to watch from the tree. After a while, when I had become accustomed to my human form, especially getting used to having legs and no longer flying, I would follow Deman to his stall and help. Deman said a lot more men seemed to stop by his stall when I was around. He didn't sound very happy about it, but he said as long as nobody touched me and they ordered something to eat or drink, he would keep his thoughts to himself.

I was not comfortable with it either. Some of the men would dilly-dally and ask me a lot of irrelevant questions before telling me their orders. Some would ask for things that were not on the menu, knowing that we wouldn't be able to make them. I found this very annoying, and sometimes I had an urge to take a knife from the kitchen and rip open the veins in their necks. But as my husband observed, they had only words to tease me; no man attempted to touch me.

I loved my husband. I had seen more beautiful men who came by our stall, but I liked the way he treated me kindly. I liked the attention he gave me. And I liked how gentle he was. But there was something missing. Or rather, I felt that I was missing something.

After a while, my stomach started to bloat, and this made my husband and the old woman very happy. We were going to have a baby. I did not really understand what was going on, but as time went by, my stomach got bigger. Several months later, after a pain I have never felt before, I gave birth to a female human baby. My mother-in-law named her Simolek.

It made everybody happy. But although the human baby was beautiful and smelled so nice, I felt a sadness within me. I didn't know why.

One night, while I was about to fall asleep with the baby suckling on my breast, I felt a tug on my big toe. It was Toyol, my old friend.

"What are you doing?" I whispered loudly.

"Hehehe … sorry … I thought of sucking a little blood," he said, feeling ashamed.

"You come near my toe, and I'll kick you," I told him.

When I saw that the baby had dozed off, I sat up on my bed. My husband was away on a fishing trip with his friends. There were only me, Simolek, and my mother-in-law, who slept on the floor in the living area. I could hear her snoring.

"How did you find me?" I asked Toyol.

He grinned and said, "I wasn't really looking for you. I was following the scent of a new-born."

"I thought you did not drink blood anymore," I said.

"You are so naïve. Fruits are nice, but I am a Toyol. I have to have blood." He sighed.

We sat quietly for a while. Toyol was eying my baby.

"You come anywhere near her, and I'll tear your head from your body."

"Can you still do that? You are human now," he asked.

"Would you like to find out?" I said, although I was not sure myself. But Toyol was convinced.

"The Djinn is looking for you," said Toyol. "He was really worried, and he's angrier all the time now. Nobody likes to be around him now. Even the Pocongs stay away from him. He has a … thing for you, I guess."

"Really? How come he hasn't found me? You did," I asked.

"He knows you are here. But I don't think he wants to come into the village. There's that shaman that can see him, and I think he's afraid of him. What about the old woman there … can I suck her blood?"

"That's my mother-in-law. She takes good care of me. And I must take good care of her. Why don't you go to the back of the house and drink some chicken blood instead," I suggested.

"I've been having chicken blood since ... forever. Are you going to stay here forever? In this village, with these humans?"

"Hmmm ... I never thought of that. But I have a daughter now. And I think I love her very much. I'll take my life one day at a time. I think she's the most beautiful thing in the world," I said to Toyol, looking at my sleeping baby. In my heart, there was that sadness again.

*****

"Who were you talking to?" my mother-in-law asked when we were at the river washing our clothes. My little baby was asleep and comfortably snuggled on my back in a batik sarong tied around my torso.

"Huh?" was my reply, as I paused from smashing and pounding my husband's pants on a smooth river rock.

"Last night," my mother-in-law continued, "I heard you talking to someone."

"Just an old friend," I said and continued my washing. I really enjoy doing the laundry. I love the sound and smell of the river, the warm morning sun on my face, the sound of birds and other fauna in the surrounding bushes, and the gentle breeze rustling the leaves above.

"I have seen him before. I know who he is," my mother-in-law said.

I paused again. The wind picked up a bit. I felt a little dismay as I looked up to see clouds building up. "He said his master was one of the villagers here, Pakji Tonel."

"Yes, Tonel. He died alone, poor thing. Both his wives left him because the … err … your friend started to suckle blood from their toes. The wives and his children only came back after we found him dead after a few days. They buried him next to his house, took all his money, and continued on with their lives in the city," my mother-in-law said, with not much real sympathy in her voice for Pakji Tonel.

We both continued on with our chores in silence. When all the washing were done, my mother-in-law got up and put the basin of washed clothes on her head. I took a pail of undergarments and walked beside her. I could tell there was something heavy on her mind.

"Are you feeling all right?" I asked her as we both walked back to our house. The baby slept on, swayed by the rhythm of my gait. "You look worried."

"I am." She stopped and turned to me. "I worry for the baby…"

*****

"Master! I found her!!" Toyol yelled as he ran towards the Djinn. "She is staying with an old woman and her little baby. Her man is not around for a few days."

"Can you go back there tonight?" asked the Djinn.

"Of course, Master," Toyol said.

"Here is what you must do … and if you do this, you can have the baby to suck blood from."

"Of course, Master," Toyol said again, smacking his lips. "I will do anything you say, Master."

"Tonight, sneak into their house while everyone is asleep. Go to her, and pull out the nail stuck at the back of her neck. That is what is keeping her in her human form. Once the nail is out, she will transform quickly back to her old self. It will be painful for her. Her craving for blood will return, and she will want to quench her thirst, which was held back for all these time. She will probably run amok for a while, terrorising and sucking the blood of the villagers. You must be quick to grab the baby if you want it for yourself. Otherwise, the baby will be her first victim," the Djinn instructed Toyol.

"She drank blood too? She said she doesn't like blood. She told me she thinks it is disgusting." Toyol remembered the times they spent perched on the tallest tree in the forest.

"Yes, she does. But every time the thirst for blood comes, she blacks out until she has satiated herself. Then she goes to sleep. When she wakes up, she does not remember a single thing that has happened."

"Will she hurt me once I pull out the nail, Master?"

"She will kill all in her path, even the baby and the old woman. You must move quickly."

This made Toyol a little nervous. But he was motivated by the thought of having the baby all to himself and getting his only real friend back. Besides, he foresaw that the task was fairly easy to execute. His biggest challenge was to ensure that Seri was really asleep.

*****

That night, I couldn't sleep. I kept waking up and worrying about the baby. But each time I was awakened, I found my baby safe and sound, snuggled up to me. Every time I saw her, I felt relieved and tried to sleep again, but then I was awoken again by some strange dream of impending danger.

The house was quiet, very quiet. I didn't even hear my mother-in-law's snoring, although I could see her outline in the flickering light of the small kerosene lamp. She was sleeping on her side, with her back to me. In the morning, my dear husband would be back. Suddenly, I missed him so much.

I closed my eyes to try to sleep again. Suddenly, I felt a stinging pain in the back of my neck. And then … nothing.

*****

The old woman tried to grab the midget ghost as he yanked the nail out from Seri's neck. But she was too late. Instead, instinctively, she grabbed the baby as Seri transformed back into her Pontianak state.

The transformation was horrible. Seri started to get into a fit. Her whole body shook and convulsed. Her beautiful skin turned pale, and her fingernails grew long and sharp. She screamed and laughed, and the old woman saw Seri's teeth grow long and jagged.

The old woman did not wait to see more. She ran as fast as her old legs could carry her, heading towards the shaman's house. The shaman's door was already open, and he was standing at the door.

No words were spoken. The shaman closed the door. Inside, there was already a congregation of people, dressed in white and chanting.

Back at the house, the transformation shocked Toyol. He was petrified. This was a side of his "friend" he had never seen before. The transformation was quick. Before Toyol could even think of running away, Seri had grabbed the top of his head with one hand and his shoulder with another. Almost casually, she separated the two. Seri was disappointed that there was no blood spewing out of the headless body. She threw the severed body aside and looked for the baby and the old woman. By that time, the old woman was already out of the door, carrying the still-sleeping baby in her arms.

Seri screamed and flew out of the house to give chase. But as she came near the shaman's house, the chanting coming from inside the house felt like a million needles stabbing her entire body.

This made her even angrier. Her thirst for blood was overwhelming. She turned away from the shaman's house, went to the nearest house, and ravaged through it. She found nobody there, or at the next house or the next.

When Seri's mother-in-law consulted the shaman about Toyol's visit, he had quickly deduced that the Djinn would ask Toyol to remove the nail from Seri's neck to return her to her original state. The old shaman had seen enough to know the horror of a Pontianak turning back from her human state. As a precaution, he asked his neighbours to evacuate their houses during the day and stay with families and friends in the other nearby villages, except those chosen ones whom the shaman picked to help repel Seri.

"Seri!" a voice suddenly rang in the still of the night. Seri stopped in her tracks.

"Seri, it is me, your husband. I have come home," Deman said.

Seri peered through a slit between two wall planks of the wooden house. There, in the light of the moon, she saw the round silhouette of a man. He stood in middle of the path leading the house, alone.

"Seri, I am back. I miss you and our daughter. I brought back your favourite fish. We can ask Mak to cook it with coconut milk and chilli and turmeric … our favourite,"

Deman appealed to Seri. Seri glided out of the house and paused at the doorway.

Deman had gone on one of his regular fishing trips on the Muar River. He and two other fellow villagers would hire a fishing boat at the jetty in Muar, about thirty kilometres away, go off for a few days, and come back with one or two Sembilang fish (salt-water catfish), Seri's favourite fish, for his mother to cook.

That day, he did not feel good and insisted that he needed to go home one day earlier than planned. His two colleagues saw his distress and agreed to cut short their trip.

By the time he reached the village, it was already dark. He could tell something was wrong. All the houses were silent and seemed abandoned. He knew that his worst fears had come true when in the distance he heard the wailing laugh of what his wife used to be. He felt fear, not of what his wife had become but for the safety of his daughter and the thought of losing his wife.

He ran to their house. He rushed inside and found the severed body of Toyol, in whose hand Deman saw the nail that he once embedded into Seri's neck to make her human. There weren't any signs of blood anywhere, which made him feel a little relieved. Maybe his mother and the baby were safe.

Then he heard Seri's eerie wailing. He prised the nail from Toyol's fingers and ran towards the sound of the laughter. He saw Seri disappearing in to one of the villager's houses.

"Seri, don't leave me. Don't leave us. We are a family. You and me and Mak and Simolek ... remember Simolek?"

Deman thought he saw Seri's mouth move, making the name of her daughter. The Pontianak stood looking directly at Deman. Then she lunged at lightning speed at Deman. As Seri was about to sink her fangs into Deman's neck to gorge on his blood, she could hear her baby crying. It sounded so close. She turned her head to look over her shoulder. Just a few yards away, her mother-in-law stood, holding her daughter in her arms.

"Here's your baby, Seri," her mother-in-law said. Then she felt the pain behind her neck. Again, the night became white. Then it was dark again.

*****

Simolek is starting to learn to roll on her belly. Every time I put her down on her back, Deman laughs to see her struggle, arms flailing for leverage, as she writhes and squirms to turn on her front. Each time she succeeds, she gives out a little chuckle, so cute and sweet, that I love so much. She is the light of our lives.

The village shaman has been paying me and the baby a visit almost every night. "Just a precaution," he says when I bluntly ask why he comes so often. I do not understand, but I do feel a sense of security when he drops by.

I had a bad dream. I could not remember any of it, but I woke up that morning with almost the same strange feeling as the time when I became human. It was almost noon when I woke up, and the first thing I saw was my husband smiling over me. There was a wonderful smell of spices and coconut milk. I knew immediately that my husband had brought home my favourite fish, and my mother-in-law was cooking my favourite dish.

Then I saw Simolek in my husband's arms. She was pushing herself against her father to get to me.

That was a few weeks ago, and my life seems more peaceful now. I do wonder about Toyol once in a while. I suppose he has found a new master, because he doesn't come around to visit me anymore. I miss him.

The shaman says everything is all right now, but he forbids me and Deman to go near a big tree at the edge of the forest reserve, at the north end of our village. It is an eerie place; nobody wants to go there, anyway. Otherwise, I have never been happier.

*****

From the tallest tree near the village, the Djinn sits on the highest branch, looking down at the daily activities of the humans below. The mid-morning sun is shining bright. He knows on days like this, she will go to the river to do her washing. She will walk to the river, her daughter snug in the sling around her slender body, her hair tied into a ponytail waving behind her, her exposed neck shining with a thin layer of sweat. At times, the sun will glint off the head of the nail just below her hairline.

The shaman has fenced up the village with his strongest magic. No Djinn or ghosts can enter. Even the blind Pocongs literally bounce off an invisible wall along the borders of this village. The Djinn can only watch from afar, at least for as long as the shaman is alive. And he's old.

"I will wait," says the Djinn to himself as he descends from the tree, once Seri is out of his sight. "I will wait, for your death."

The Bunian Nobleman

Sani was once abducted by spirits known as Bunians (pronounced "BOO-nee-ahns"). The Bunians live in the jungles of Malaysia and are invisible, except to those chosen ones who are able to see the spirit world. They are benevolent spirits, known to have taken into their care many who were lost in the jungle. Those taken in by the Bunians rarely want to leave, for theirs is a beautiful world, and they are beautiful people. Men taken in by the Bunian will not be able to resist the beautiful Bunian women, and many will forget the wife and children they left behind in the human world once smitten by a Bunian beauty.

But there are those who miss the human world and ask to be sent home. If their wish is granted, usually they will awake to find themselves at the edge of the jungle, near their village. And in all cases, although they felt they were only gone for a short time and they have hardly aged, the people that they knew in the village are either very old or have died.

That must have happened to Sani. One day he wandered into the village and asked the villagers about his mother, his father, and his relatives. None of the villagers could recall any of the names he mentioned until a very old resident said that the names sounded familiar, but all of them were now inscribed on tombstones in the old cemetery.

He cried realising that his loved ones were gone. He asked the villagers if his family house was still standing and who now lived there. The villagers took him to the old house they believed once belonged to the deceased family. It had been empty since the last occupant – an elderly woman who lived alone after the death of her husband five years earlier – died about a year or so ago. She had a son, her only child, but he had abandoned her ever since he married a city girl.

"Yes," Sani told the villagers, "this is indeed the house in which I grew up. Thank you, kind people of my village. At last I am home."

He settled himself down in the old house and made some repairs with the help of the villagers. They started a collection for Sani and bought building material to fix the house.

The villagers were concerned for Sani. They gave him some more money to start his new life and donated bags of rice, flour, sugar, and salt and even a chicken for him to slaughter and eat for his sustenance. The imam, with the help his connections within the local authorities, even arranged for the reconnection of running water and electricity to the old house.

The imam of the village mosque later thought that, instead of hiring contract cleaners, he could ask Sani to work as janitor and groundskeeper for the little mosque, if Sani was agreeable. Of course, he was. He thanked the imam and the villagers profusely. They felt pity for him, a man suddenly finding himself alone in a familiar world in an unfamiliar time.

About a week after his reappearance, Sani seemed to have adapted to life in the present time. He had kept himself busy, either at the mosque by cleaning the toilets, sweeping the grounds, and clearing the weeds in the graveyard or at his new home by repairing, putting in new fixtures, and rebuilding.

Then one night, after the night prayer at the mosque, a villager was bold enough to ask him about the time he disappeared. All of them had been curious, but they were nice people who did not want to impose themselves on him as he was still adjusting himself to his new life.

He obliged and invited the villager to come to his house. But the word that Sani was ready to tell his amazing story spread so quickly that by the time he settled himself down to start his story, it looked as if the whole village had congregated on his front porch. He smiled to all of them. He apologised that he could not let them into his old house, for fear that it could not take the weight of the gathering crowd, or offer them any form of refreshments, as is customary for Malays when receiving guests. They all said "Don't worry about it" in unison.

He sat on the threshold of his house, at the top of a five-step green cement staircase, facing his audience. Some of them sat on the stairs just below him; others either made themselves comfortable on the wooden bench that Sani had built, which accommodated six comfortably, or just stood around the porch. Some went home and came back with several plastic chairs.

Sani invited the elderly and the imam into the house. His neighbour, Pak Yahya, shouted from his house not to start without him and came with his wife and daughter, carrying a tray full of the leftover traditional goodies from his little food stall and two kettles of black coffee. His two sons carried two collapsible tables, which they quickly set up to hold the goodies and drinks.

Sani laughed at the industry put in by these generous village people.

"Thank you all," Sani started, and the buzz and chatter quieted down immediately.

Sani started from the day he left this house. It was a beautiful morning. He remembered there were rumours thick in the air that soon the British would grant independence to the Federation of Malaya. But as for Sani, he was concerned only of one thing; his marriage to a local girl by the name of Hasnah binti Abu Leman.

The villagers gasped. That was the name of the old lady who lived here in this house. Sani held back his emotions when he heard this. He told the villagers that Hasnah was the love of his life. They had known each other since they were children. After he graduated from a teachers college up north, he was offered a job in Sitiawan, Perak. Afraid of losing her to another man, he proposed to her. To his delight, she accepted, and the wedding was set to be held a year later. The wedding never took place, of course, since he went missing soon after starting work.

"But how come she was living in my family house?" Sani was curious after he composed himself.

"I remember," said an old lady sitting in a corner chewing on betel leaves. "After you disappeared, she was so distressed that she kept herself away from society. But the wedding arrangements were already made. Your elder brother … what's his name?"

"Sabri?" Sani said.

"Yes, Sabri. He was a teacher at the religious school in Muar town. He was the shy type and had always asked for your mother to find a wife for him," the old woman recalled. "My father was the imam at that time, and he suggested that your brother marry Hasnah. She was reluctant at first, but everybody thought it was a good idea. So she relented. She bore one son, but he turned out to be a useless fellow. He joined a rock group, became famous, married a stewardess, and never came back to this village after that."

"Ya Allah, how sad. It is written that she is to marry my brother," Sani said, burying his face in his hands again.

The villagers sitting near him rubbed his back. The others shook their heads in sympathy. Then one of them urged him to tell his story.

On a weekend a few days before Independence, in August 1957, he and a few friends decided to go picnicking at a place called the Burmese Pool, a rock pool at the foot of Maxwell Hill in Taiping Perak.

They frolicked in the water, climbed on slippery rocks, and explored the surrounding rainforest. It was fun. Just a little after noon, they found a nice shady spot, upstream and away from the crowd, laid out a *mengkuang* (screw pine) mat, and sat down on it to have lunch. They had prepared, to best of their abilities, *nasi lemak* (white rice cooked in coconut milk) with fresh cucumber slices, small fried anchovies, roasted peanuts, half a hard-boiled egg, and *sambal tumis* (hot spicy sauce), all wrapped up in banana leaves. Swimming always made you hungry. Nobody complained about the food, and they ate heartily. It was a sumptuous meal that made Sani sleepy. His friends wanted to go a bit further, up to where there was a small waterfall, but Sani felt too sleepy and lethargic. He told them that he needed to take a nap and would join them in fifteen minutes. His friends left him leaning against a shady tree, and almost immediately he fell asleep.

A drop of rain woke him up. When he opened his eyes, the skies had darkened, big drops of rain were starting to fall, and the wind whistled through the trees as the foliage rustled. Sani got up and started to call out to his friends. He gathered his things and saw that his friends' bags and shoes, were not there. They must have taken them with when they went up to the waterfall. He called out their names and, hugging his bag and shoes, started walking the way his friends went. When he reached the waterfall, no one was there. He called out their names. His voice echoed throughout the forest, but he did not get a reply.

Sani could not find them. All their things were gone, and for a while he thought they were playing a trick on him. But as the rain started to pour, he had no choice but to find his way back out to where their car was parked.

He walked down the trail that was supposed to lead him out. But though he felt he was walking a long time, still he was nowhere near the clearing to the main street. The rain was getting heavier, and there were thunder and lightning. He decided to stop for a while to get his bearings. He then realised that he couldn't hear the sound of the river. He was sure the trail was never far from the river and thus, it should be very much within earshot, even though he couldn't see it anymore. He decided to go back to the riverside. Maybe that would give him a better idea of where he was.

That was when he saw one of his friends on the other side of the rushing river. He was waving and saying something. His voice was drowned out by the sound of the rain on the trees and the roar of the rushing water between them. Sani looked up and down the river for a place to cross. He saw a huge boulder jutting out of the water just upriver. It looked like he could jump onto it from this side and then make a slightly longer leap to the other side. The water was strong, and the boulder was slippery, but he made it across. When he arrived at the place where he thought his friend was, he could not find anybody.

It was getting dark, and Sani realised that he was lost. He kept walking downriver, but he had a strange feeling that he was passing by the same trees and rock formations.

The rain began to let up, but by that time it was totally dark. Wet and cold, he began to feel tired and hungry. Finally, he sat down underneath a clump of bamboo plant. Then he saw a white-shrouded figure coming towards him. As it came nearer, he was convinced that it was a Pontianak, coming for his blood. He closed his eyes and waited for the end but felt a soft hand touching his head instead. He looked up, and the most beautiful woman he had ever seen in his life was smiling down on him. She started to walk away from him. Then she turned around and beckoned him to follow.

Sani stopped telling his story. It was getting late, and he told those staring at him with mouths agape that he was feeling tired and had his chores to do before the dawn prayers at the mosque. Therefore, he said he would very much like to continue the story the next day. They sighed in unison but acceded that they too were getting tired and sleepy. The villagers got up and started walking back to their homes, excitedly discussing with each other what they had just heard and eagerly awaiting the remaining story. Sani helped Pak Yahya with the collapsible tables and helped him carry the empty kettles back to his house.

The next morning after the morning prayers and the morning sermon, Sani asked the imam if he could go to town. "Of course," the imam said. "Why not?"

Sheepishly, Sani admitted that he had never learned how to drive a car. A motorcycle he might be able to handle, but even so, he would not know where to go.

"Ooh, I understand. Sahak! Sahak!" the good imam shouted. He was calling after a man who was passing by. Sahak was on a motorcycle with a rectangular metal sidecar filled with vegetables, some local fruits, tapioca, sweet potatoes, and a few bags of rice. Sahak was the village grocer, who apparently had just come from town for supplies to replenish the stocks at his little grocery and convenience store a few hundred meters from the mosque.

Sahak stopped and turned into the mosque compound.

"Assalamu'alaikum, Imam. What can I get you?" Sahak said, not dismounting.

"Wa'alaikumsalam, Sahak," the imam answered Sahak's greeting, raising his voice above the puttering of Sahak's motorcycle. "Nothing for me. But our friend here wants to go see the town. If your son is not busy, can you let him take Sani to town? He passed his driving test last month, didn't he?"

Sani looked a little concerned when he heard that his possible chauffeur, had just passed his driving test. The imam saw it in his face and laughed.

"Don't worry, Sani. The boy is a better driver than me. He's been driving since he was twelve," the imam said with a laugh.

"Yes, of course," Sahak said. "He'll jump at the opportunity."

"Thank you, Sahak. I'll go home to change, and then I'll go to your shop," Sani said as he hurried off home.

It was almost nine in the morning when Sani reached Sahak's little shop. His son was sitting on a small stool and scraping out coconut flesh using the scraping machine. "Abah, Pak Sani is here!" he shouted. His hair and body were covered in tiny coconut scrapings.

Sahak came out from the dark interior of his little shop. He asked his son to change. The boy got up and ran across the small village road to their house. Sahak offered Sani a cigarette and invited him to sit on a plastic chair he pulled from inside the shop. Sani declined the cigarette but accepted the chair.

"So what are you planning to do in town?" Sahak was curious.

"I just want to see how much it has changed. The last time I went to town, I took a trishaw from here to the river, then a boat across the river, and then another trishaw to the town centre," recalled Sani.

"Oh, we have a bridge now," Sahak told Sani. "When were you born?"

"In 1933. My father could not remember exactly when I was born. But he said it was during the rainy season, so it must be in November or December," Sani said, shrugging his shoulders.

"That means you are seventy years old," Sahak said after a quick mental calculation.

"How long did it feel to you, staying with *them*?" Sahak asked further, flicking his head to one side.

"I don't really know. It felt like maybe ten years, maybe fifteen the most. I wanted to leave. I missed my parents. But I was torn between the family I had there and the family I left behind," Sani said with a far-away look in his eyes. Sahak thought he saw tears welling up in Sani's eyes.

"You got married? To a Bunian?" Sahak asked in awe. "Was she beautiful?"

"Yes, she was the most beautiful woman I have ever seen …"

Sahak was waiting for more details about Sani's beautiful wife, but Sani did not say anything further.

"OK, I'm ready. Let's go!" Zul, Sahak's son, surprised them both.

"Have you got the car key?" Sahak asked Zul.

"Yes," Zul said holding the key in the air by its key-chain.

"OK. Drive carefully. Here's money for petrol. Don't come home too late," Sahak said. He patted Sani on his back and went back inside his little shop.

"Come, Pak Sani. The car is there," Zul said, pointing to a shed. From where Sani was, he can see a shiny gold 1984 Toyota Cressida.

"Wah, what a beautiful car! Is it new?" Sani was impressed.

"Hahaha, well, it's new to us. We just bought it from a used car dealer in town about a month ago. But this is a fifteen-year-old model," explained Zul. "Come, get in. Let's go to town!"

Sani opened the door and sat in the front passenger seat. Zul reversed the car expertly and drove off, honking a good-bye to his father, who acknowledged them with a nod. The imam was right about how good a driver Zul was. He drove neither too fast nor too slow. Sani enjoyed the ride, taking in the sights and sounds of a modern world alien to him. They did not say much to each other as they made their way to town. Sani became excited as they approach the bridge, where people and vehicles used to board the ferry to cross the river. Zul obliged Sani with a brief history of the Sultan Ismail Bridge: completed in early 1960s, officiated in 1967, every year the bridge will ask for a life, so there will always be somebody compelled to jump off the top of the arc. Sani thought Zul was exaggerating. Zul said just last month, somebody told his friend that a woman took a taxi from her house and asked the driver to stop at the top of the bridge, where she got off, climbed over the railing, and jumped into the water. They never found the body.

They drove around Muar Town rather aimlessly. Zul first went to the town centre and drove along the main road.

Then he made a full circle past the taxi and bus stop, the town council, and the bridge to the other bus and taxi stand toward the hospital. Then he turned around again and onto the main road. Instead of making another round, Zul took Sani to Tanjung Emas (Golden Cape), where he parked. They both took a walk near the waterfront where the Muar River meets the Straits of Melaka.

"Everything must look very different to you," Zul said after he ordered some Mee Rojak from the Indian Muslim seller who had his wares on the back of his bicycle.

"Yes," Sani said, looking out to sea. "This is all new to me. I am in a foreign land."

"Do you miss your ... er ... old place?"

"Yes, I do. I think about it every day." Sani looked sad.

"Then why did you leave?" Zul asked.

"I had to," Sani said, and then he went quiet.

After they had their Mee Rojak and cold drinks from another food vendor, Sani asked Zul if he could drive back to town. He needed to buy some books and stationery.

"Are you going back to school?" Zul teased him.

"No. I need to write down some things ... I may be going back," Sani said seriously.

"Going back?" Zul did not understand.

"I don't belong here," Sani said as he stood up from the concrete parapet that separated the tarmac pedestrian walk and the lazy river flowing out to sea. "Come, let's go."

Zul took him to a popular book shop in Muar, but Sani wanted to go to one particular one, which he said he had seen while they were sightseeing around town earlier. Zul knew about the shop. It wasn't really a book shop but a shop selling art supplies. Sani asked Zul to wait in the car, since he wouldn't be long. Anyway, there wasn't any available parking space.

Zul sat in the car and saw Sani going inside the shop. Sani spoke to the shop assistant. She went to the back and then returned with an elderly Chinese man, whom Zul recognised as the shop owner. Once, some time ago, Zul had gone to this shop to get paints and manila cardboard to make some advertising posters for his father's shop in the village. At that time, the elderly man was in the shop. The old man told Zul stand outside the shop while he was getting the things Zul needed. He told Zul, "I don't want you to steal things in my shop."

Zul had hated the old man and vowed never to come to the shop again. He told his father, and his father said he knew about the old Chinese shop owner. Sahak said not to think about it too much. The old man just did not like Malays. There were rumours that he had once been a Communist Party leader, but this was just hearsay. Looking inside from the car, Zul saw Sani talking to the old man. The old man listened intently and, to his surprise, put a hand on Sani's shoulders. He nodded, understanding what Sani was saying. Then the old man went back to the rear of the shop. Sani turned to the shop assistant, who had been standing behind him all the while, and said something to her. She got him a notebook and a pen or maybe a mechanical pencil. She put them in a plastic bag and gave them to Sani. Sani said good-bye or something to her, and she waved back. Zul did not see Sani pay for the items he bought.

Sani went back into the car. "Come, let's go home," Sani said, smiling to Zul. Zul smiled back, put the car in gear, and drove off. The trip home was quiet, with both driver and passenger lost in their own thoughts. After Zul parked the car back under the shed at his house, they got out of the car. Sani said thank you, and Zul just gave a nod. Sani went back to his house. Zul went into his house, changed, and went across the road to his father's grocery shop to carry on with his daily chores.

That night, as promised, the village people congregated at Sani's house after the night prayers. It looked like the whole village was there, more than the night before. Pak Yahya catered just as he had the night before.

Once Sani took his place at the top of the cement stairs, everybody quieted down, eagerly awaiting the second and, hopefully, final part of the story of Sani's life in the Bunian world.

"The beautiful woman, did she become your wife?" someone asked.

"Hahaha," Sani laughed. "No, actually she became my mother-in-law."

There was a gasp.

Sani got up to his feet and followed the beautiful woman, keeping some distance between them. She seemed to be glowing in the dark. They walked a long way along a trail Sani was sure, hadn't been there before. Finally, they reached a village. The dense jungle just suddenly ended, and Sani was walking along a path with houses on both sides. There were no street lights, but at certain intervals, there were torches burning atop wooden poles. There wasn't anybody outside. Sani presumed they were all inside their houses. It was night-time, after all.

The woman turned into a path leading to one of the houses. Like the houses in Sani's own village, it was built on stilts some four feet off the ground, but it was more old-fashioned than what Sani was used to. In Sani's village, the stairs leading up the front door were all cement; there, they were more like wooden ladders.

The woman stopped before climbing up the stairs to wash her feet. There was an earthenware crock just next to the stairs. She opened the lid, and Sani saw it was filled with water. The woman took a coconut shell skewered with bamboo, which was leaning against the crock, scooped water from the crock, and poured it over her lovely feet. Sani noticed she was barefooted. She looked at Sani and then signalled him to take off his shoes and wash his feet. Then she went up the stairs, pushed the front door open, and called out to somebody. She spoke Malay, but with a rather old-fashioned diction, much like the way old Malay literature was written.

Sani sat on the lowest rung of the stairs. He took off the slippers he had on. They were all muddied, as were parts of his feet up to his ankles. He started to wash his feet with the water from the crock. While he was doing that, rubbing and scraping off the mud with his hands, he felt someone tapping his shoulder. He looked up behind him. The woman was at the door, showing him a pile of clean clothes.

"When you are done, please bathe and change into these. The bathroom is behind the house," she said in her strange Malay dialect.

The bathroom was a structure separate from the main house and was really a shed built around a well. The water was cold and refreshing. Sani put on the clothes he was given, a shirt with no buttons he had to slip over his head and a sarong.

As he stepped out of the bathroom, he was surprised by a man who was standing outside the bathroom, apparently waiting for him to finish. He smiled at Sani and pointed to Sani's soiled shirt, pants, and underpants, which he had rolled up into a ball and was holding with both hands, wondering where he could keep them safe for the night. He planned to wash them the next day. Once they dried, he could put them back on, thank his host, and find his way back to Taiping.

The man, seeing that Sani was reluctant to part with his laundry, reached for the ball of clothes. Sani quickly hide the clothes behind his back. The man chased after it, going behind Sani, and Sani kept the clothes away from him by passing them around his body. This went on for three complete rounds until one of the windows of the house opened and the beautiful woman looked down upon Sani and the strange man. She smiled.

"He is my man-servant, sir. Please give your dirty clothes to him. He will have them cleaned for you. Please come up to the house. We have prepared a meal for you," said the woman.

Sani was hungry. He gave the man his clothes and walked to the front of the house. Another woman was at the door, younger than the one before and just as beautiful, if not more. She invited Sani into the house. Inside, on the floor of the living area(there was no furniture), laid out on a big white piece of cloth, there was a spread of rice, stir-fried vegetables, fish in red gravy, and slices of mango and watermelon. It smelled good. Sani maintain his composure, but his stomach gave out a low rumble. He felt embarrassed. The younger woman gave out a little laugh and disappeared behind curtains which divided the living area into the dining area and what looked to Sani like another lounging area. Through the occasional gaps created by people walking through the curtain, Sani saw and heard casual conversations spattered with low laughter.

A rather elderly man, perhaps in his early fifties, pushed aside the curtain and smiled at Sani. Sani was still standing near the front door, trying to fathom the difference between the small house he had seen from outside and the vast space he was seeing inside. The man introduced himself as Nila. Behind him stood the beautiful woman who had led Sani to this place. The man introduced the woman as Merah, his wife.

"Come, let us eat. I myself have not had dinner. Come, sit next to me," Nila said to Sani.

Sani sat down, and Nila sat beside him. Merah scooped rice from the bowl and served some to Sani and then to Nila. Sani could see there were two others in the lounge area behind the curtain.

Sani did not think any more of them. He was hungry. He remained polite and composed, but he had three plates of rice, and his host had to ask for a refill of the red gravy and the fish in it. After dinner, Sani was invited to sit together with the other two men in the lounge. They all sat on the wooden floor, the men in lotus position and Merah with both legs folded to her right side. The two men did not really talk to Sani, but Sani saw they were observing him intently. Sani felt uncomfortable but manage to carry on a conversation with the host, Nila, and Merah. They asked about him, his family, and how he ended up in that part of the jungle. Sani told them about his picnic and how his friends had abandoned him, although he did not understand why. When he mentioned this, the two men shook their heads.

In turn, the hosts, Nila and Merah, told them about their village. The village was known as Kampung Ayer Putih. Sitting with them were the two men Tarum and Rintek. Tarum and Rintek, apparently, did not approve of Merah bringing Sani back to their village and expressed this to Nila and Merah as if Sani wasn't there. All four of them started to argue. Sani felt guilty and sat there quietly as the debate raged on. In the midst of that, Sani actually dozed off and started snoring. His snoring woke him up, and as he looked up, he saw everyone looking at him. Merah was the only one smiling. She said Sani must be very tired after the day's ordeal and called the servant who had taken Sani's clothes earlier. She called him Jadam. Sani got up, apologised to the host and to the two angry men, and followed Jadam.

Jadam took Sani out the front door and to another house maybe fifty metres away. The night was cool. Sani could hear the sounds of the river flowing, an owl hooting, and crickets. The sky was a little overcast, but Sani could see the new moon floating in and out of moving clouds. They came upon a smaller house, a guest house, Sani presumed, that was built on stilts in a similar design to the hosts' house. Inside, through the already opened door, Sani saw a mattress wrapped in a white bed sheet, pillows in white pillowcases, lamps in every corner, giving a low glow, and a bowl of incense permeating the room with a lovely, relaxing smell.

Sani washed his feet and climbed the three rungs up to a small patio. Jadam followed him to the door, and as soon as Sani was inside, Jadam asked if Sani need anything else. Sani said no, he would like to sleep. Jadam bowed his head and closed the door. Sani laid himself down on the mattress and immediately fell asleep.

The next morning, Sani was awakened by the sound of a soft knocking on the door. When he opened his eyes, he did not know where he was for a few seconds. The soft knocking sounded again, and Sani sat up on his mattress and called out, "Yes?"

"It me, Jadam, sir. My master and mistress would like for you to join them for breakfast, sir," said a voice from behind the door.

"All right, Jadam. But I would like to wash up a bit," Sani said.

"Of course, sir. There is a change of clothes in the little cupboard, sir. You may wash yourself in the bathroom behind the house," Jadam replied.

"Thank you, Jadam. I will be there in about fifteen minutes," Sani estimated.

"I beg your pardon, sir?"

"I'll be there. Give me some time," Sani said. He got up, went to the little cupboard as described by Jadam, and found another set of clothes that was exactly like the one he was wearing. He took the clothes with him and went out a back door that led outside to another patio, this one without any roof or railing and not more than four or five feet wide. There were stairs on the right side leading down to another structure, which Sani recognised as the bathroom.

The morning was beautiful. The sky was bright, although the sun had not come up over the trees surrounding the village. The chirping birds, the distant sound of the river, and the cool morning breeze were refreshing. Sani pushed aside the heavy cloth covering the entrance to the bathroom. Inside was a well surrounded by a wall made of palm fronds. There was a damp cloth hanging on the wall of the well, which Sani knew was the bathing cloth. Under these conditions, one was not expected to bathe in the nude.

After Sani finished bathing, changed into his new clothes, and even brushed his teeth with a twig with a frayed end, he stepped out of the bathroom and was again surprised by Jadam, who was waiting for Sani to give him the clothes he had worn last night. This time he gave them up readily. Sani went up into the house to make up his bed but found it was already made up. So he went out the front door, and Jadam was there too, waiting to lead him back to his master's house.

There were no clocks anywhere in the village. During the day, time was measured by the position of the sun. The people would make appointments or set deadlines by saying, for example, "I will meet you here tomorrow morning when the sun just appear over the trees" or "when the sun is overhead". At night, time was measured by their biological clock. Most of them would be inside before sunset.

Three days past, but his host had not mentioned or suggested that he should be sent back home. Sani wanted to go home. As wonderful as life was there, Sani missed his mother. For the last three days he had been taken on a tour of different parts of the village. The first day after breakfast, Nila, with Jadam, took Sani on a bullock cart ride to their fruit orchard, where there were rows of durian trees, rambutan trees, mangosteen trees, and an assortment of many other fruit trees, all laden with fruit. They spent the whole day picking fruits and eating them. Jadam brought some lunch. They came back to Nila's house just before sunset.

The second day, Merah asked if Sani would like to join her and Jadam on their weekly trip to the market. Again, they spent the whole day there. Merah bought a lot of things, although Sani did not really see her paying for any of the things she purchased. All the sellers treated like royalty.

The third day, Nila took Sani hunting. They brought back several birds and a mousedeer. Another day passed.

On the fourth day, after breakfast with his hosts, Sani gathered the courage to ask if someone from the village could show him the way back home or at the very least to the river, from which he was sure he could find his own way back.

Nila smiled at this request. "I know you miss your home. We are trying to entertain you as much as we can so you won't think about your world so much," he said.

"My world?" Sani was astounded.

"Yes. You are in our world. This world is invisible to humans. This world occupies a huge area and a small one at the same time," Nila said, trying to make Sani understand. "Listen, you can hear the sound of the river?"

"Yes, that means we are near it," Sani said, sounding annoyed.

"Yes. For the last three days you have travelled to different parts of our world, our orchards, our market, and our hunting ground. All the while, you can always hear the river."

Now that Nila mentioned it, Sani realised how true his words were. No matter how far he travelled, it always sounded like the river was nearby.

"This is hard for you to understand. But there is one thing you must know. The door between our worlds will only open when the circumstances are right," Nila said, starting to sound more serious.

"What circumstance?" Sani began to sound panicky.

"We don't really know. We think it has something to do with the moon and the stars, because the door only opens at night," Merah jumped in. "And most of the time, we find the door by chance."

"Like that night when you found me?"

"Yes," Merah said. "I like taking a look around in your world. Maybe I am just curious. But time runs so fast in your world. Every time I find a door and take a look around your world, it has changed so much."

"When was the last time the door opened, before three days ago?" Sani was afraid to hear the answer.

"I cannot remember exactly, but maybe ten fruit seasons ago," Merah said.

Ten fruit seasons. Sani knew that there were only one or two fruit seasons in a year. "How do you know where to find the door?"

"We don't know," replied Merah. "It was just a gut feeling. I can feel it."

These were not the words of comfort Sani was looking for.

"So you were there for ten years?" asked Pak Yahya, the kuih seller.

"I don't know. Maybe. Like I said, there weren't any clocks in their world. I counted the days for a while, but I lost count," Sani explained to his audience. "My fellow villagers, why don't we continue tomorrow?" Sani announced, as he himself was starting to feel sleepy.

There was a unanimous groan from the villagers, but they all knew that Sani was right. Some of them had actually fallen asleep.

"Let's meet again here tomorrow night. Same time," Sani called out to everyone as they shuffled off. The old folks who were in the house were helped down the stairs, and soon Sani was left alone again. He locked up and went to bed.

The next day, after he finished his chores at the mosque, Sani went to see Sahak at his shop. He needed to take another trip to Muar town, to that shop he had visited yesterday. Sani said he bought something, but it was wrong and he needed to have it exchanged.

Sahak called out to Zul and asked him to give Sani a ride into town. Sahak also had some things for Zul to pick up at the wet market. Zul appeared at the window of his house, looking like he had just woken up. Zul asked Sani to wait while he washed up and changed.

The ride to town was quiet. Maybe Zul was still feeling sleepy. Zul dropped Sani at the art supply shop, and he went on to do his errands at the wet market. When he came back to fetch Sani, he saw Sani and the old man chatting and laughing. This was a rare sight as far as the grumpy old Chinese shop owner was concerned.

They went straight home – no more sightseeing. Sani helped Zul carry the things he bought from the car to Sahak's shop and said his thanks to both of them before going back home. Zul noted there some distress in Sani's face and demeanour.

For the rest of the day, Sani busied himself with his daily chores around the mosque. He even cleaned the ablution area, which he was supposed to do once a week, though he had just done so the day before yesterday.

That night after prayers, the villagers assembled again at Sani's house, eager to listen to the rest of his adventure in land of the Bunian.

Since he could not possibly find his way home, Sani accepted that this place, wherever or whenever it was, would be his home. It wasn't bad. He practically had Jadam as his personal servant, and his hosts treated him well. Merah and Nila were noble people of this land. Nila was a member of a council of sorts that administered the Bunian community. Tarum, Rintek, and seven others made up the ten-man assembly that met once every two full moons to discuss political and administrative issues.

One day, after what seemed like a week since his arrival, Sani became so bored that he finally decided to go to the hosts' house to ask Nila if he could work at one of his orchards. Sani said he wanted to earn his keep. He felt he had been living off the good graces of Nila and Merah, and he wanted to be useful, since he had no other place to go.

Nila laughed. "Now this is an honest man!" he said, putting one hand around Sani's shoulder. Sani did not know why Nila found his request for employment amusing, nor did Nila explained why. Nila took him into a room. It had no windows but was sufficiently ventilated by the wooden latticework grille at the top of all four walls, below the wooden beams supporting the roof trusses.

"Here, Sani. You look like a learned man. Our scribe has passed on several moons ago, and we can find no one to do this work. I have been filling in, but this is a full-time duty, and I cannot focus on doing it only. So the recordings of the transactions are not up to date," Nila said. He extended his arm and swept it across the room, presenting to Sani shelves full of scrolls. They were neatly stacked in a certain order, with Arabic numerals written on each scroll.

"What is this?" Sani asked, wondering if he should not have asked for things to do.

"These scrolls record our harvest: how much was harvested, how much was distributed, and how much we much keep," Nila explained.

"Your accounting records, then?"

"Eh? No, these are the things we need to make sure everybody is well fed. Nobody is hungry here," Nila said proudly.

Sani looked around the room. His predecessor, should he agree to accept this job, had been an organised person.

Everything seemed to be where it was supposed to be. In the middle of the room was a small platform elevated about one foot above the floor, which functioned, presumably, as a desk. A parchment was stretched over the surface with some writing on one side.

Sani stepped forward and kneeled down to take a closer look at the stretch parchment. The writing was in Jawi, the Malay language written in the Arabic alphabet. At the top of the parchment was the word 'Paddy'. Sani saw the word 'moon', with numbers below it. Across from it were numbers under the word 'sacks', and across from that was a name. Apparently, this was the stock record for sacks of paddy distributed to the people of this community.

"Where is the warehouse?" Sani asked Nila, who was looking around the room as if he himself were there for the first time.

"Huh? Warehouse?" Nila seemed confused.

"The place where you keep the paddy?" Sani elaborated.

"Oh! The shed," Nila said, pointing to a direction to his left. "Come, I'll show you."

Nila put his hand around Sani again and led him out of the house. They walked maybe half a mile to another big house. This was also elevated, but when Sani wanted to take off his slippers, Nila shook a finger at him. Nila climbed the steps up to the front door and knocked.

"Who is it?" asked a voice from inside.

"It is me, Nila!"

The door opened, and the man inside stood aside to let Nila in and bowed. Nila stepped over the threshold and beckoned Sani in. Again, Sani was amazed by how the size of the building from outside belied the space inside.

"Here is all the food we need to keep everybody well-fed," Nila said. "See that basket?"

Nila pointed to a basket next to the man who had opened the door for them, who was by then sitting solemnly in a lotus position behind the door. They both got closer to the man and his basket. Inside the basket were a few smooth river rocks, each carved with an Arabic numeral.

"The people here can only get one sack of paddy in one moon. One household, one sack. Usually, in the morning after the night of the full moon, the head of each household will gather at my house to get one of these rocks from the scribe. He will put down their names and then give them a rock. They take the rock and bring it to our friend here, who will take the rock and give a sack of paddy to the household leader," Nila explained.

"That is very clever. It is a very good system you have here." Sani was impressed. "But where are the paddy fields that produce all this?"

"For now, you don't worry about that, my young friend. For now, you help me with the books of the paddy, to make sure everybody here gets to eat," Nila said, grinning.

"Did you ever get to see the paddy fields?" a voice asked from near the bottom of the steps.

"No. Nila, Merah, and everyone else I asked about the paddy fields said more or less what Nila said: that I don't have to worry about it," Sani answered.

"So that was your job in their world?" asked another voice from the crowd.

"Yes, it was. It kept me quite busy. At first it was only the paddy stock I was asked to record, but then there were other grains I was asked to account for. I kept track of wheat, corn, and glutinous rice. But these did not move as fast as the paddy."

"You said the other night that the beautiful woman became your mother-in-law. You married Nila's daughter?" asked a woman's voice.

"Yes, but it was really a punishment for their daughter. The daughter had fallen in love with a boy from another Bunian community. Unfortunately, this other community was considered of a higher caste than the community I was living with. The other community warned Nila and the other council members that if Nila's daughter, Unggu, continued to seduce their boy, they would attack and burn down Nila's village. In a fit of rage, Nila asked the other council members to bear witness that he had betrothed his daughter to me and that we were to be married at the next full moon. And we were," Sani said. His voice softened when he thought about his wedding day.

"Did you have any children?" asked another woman's voice. This time the voice came from behind him, from one of the elderly ladies who were given the privilege to sit inside.

"Yes, we had two children. The first one was a boy and the second a girl," Sani said, followed with a melancholy sigh. "At first the marriage was hell. My wife refused to accept me and did not want to sleep in the same bed with me. One day, word was sent that the boy of the other community had married a woman of his parents' choice. She was broken-hearted, and I stood by her. Finally, she accepted that this was her fate. I love her. I wonder what she's doing now."

"Then why did you leave?" Sahak asked. He was sitting just one step below Sani, facing the crowd.

"I didn't want to. Just like Merah said, the window between our world and theirs would appear anywhere within a ten-year cycle. One night, a week or so ago, something woke me up in the middle of the night." Sani tried recalling the exact sequence of events.

Now that he thought about it, the thing that woke him up was the sound of thunder. But apparently it was inside his head, since his wife, who was sleeping soundly next to him, did not stir. *Must have been a dream then,* Sani thought. He sat up on his kapok-stuffed mattress and suddenly felt he needed to empty his bladder. He took one of the oil lamps on the wall and walked blearily to the back door. It was a full moon night, which meant that tomorrow would be a busy day for him, distributing the paddy to the people.

He suspected nothing amiss until he stepped out of the toilet and found himself by the river. It took him some time to realise that he was at the very place where Merah had found him a few years ago. He turned around, expecting to go back into the toilet, but behind him, under the moonlight, all he could see were just the rainforest and, beyond that, the darkness of the night.

"How did you get here?" asked another voice from the porch.

"I followed the river downstream until I ended up at the main road. By that time it was already dawn, and a lorry driver was kind enough to give me a ride. He took me to Taiping town and gave me some money. I bought a bus ticket to Muar and got another ride from another lorry driver. I asked him to drop me off at the Kampung Tanjung Gading Mosque. He knew exactly where it is, and that's when you all found me," Sani said, sounding a little sad. "I think it's getting late. Let's continue this tomorrow."

The village folks agreed and gradually dispersed.

The next morning, before dawn, Sani went to the mosque. As usual, the imam was already there, since he did not trust anybody else with the key to the front gate and the main entrance of the village mosque. That morning, the imam looked a little distraught.

"What's wrong, Imam?" Sani asked as he approached the imam, who seemed unsure about opening the gate.

"Shhh!" the imam replied, with an index finger over his puckered lips. Then, with the same finger, the imam pointed in the direction of the mosque. In the low street light, Sani could barely make out the silhouette of someone sleeping, in a foetal position, on the floor of the five-foot tiled area between the front steps and the main door.

"Who is that?" Sani asked.

"How should I know?" said the imam, clearly irritated by the presence of a stranger in his mosque. "Get Sahak and his son, Zul. And where's the bilal?"

"Here he comes," Sani pointed out the bilal, who was cycling up to the both of them.

"Why are we not inside?" asked the bilal. "It's almost time for azan."

"Shhhh!" said the imam and Sani.

"Bilal, lend me your bicycle. I need to go to Sahak's house to get him and his boy here," Sani said in a whisper to the still-bemused Bilal. Sahak was a police retiree. The villagers always called him in this type of situations.

Bilal nodded his head and passed the handlebars of his bicycle to Sani. Sani cycled as fast as he could to Sahak's house. Sahak was an early riser. He was already in his shop, taking stock of what perishables to buy today.

"Sahak, there's an intruder in our mosque. Please come and take a look," Sani almost shouted the minute he saw Sahak.

"Intruder? Allah forgive us. Wait here. I'll wake Zul up." Sahak scuttled off across the road into his house and came back again with a shotgun in his hand.

Sani was a little uncomfortable seeing Sahak slinging the gun across his torso, but he said nothing. A few seconds later, Zul appeared behind him with dishevelled hair, having not fully shaken the sleep off himself.

Sani rode back to the mosque. Sahak and Zul took Sahak's motorcycle and sped off ahead. By the time Sani reached the mosque, the front gate was already opened, and the lights outside and inside the mosque were already switched on. The loudspeaker made a wailing sound as it was turned on. This was followed by the sound of the bilal clearing his throat, preparing himself to make the call for the dawn prayer.

Sani parked the bilal's bike under the bicycle shed. As he walked toward the mosque's entrance, he noticed someone at the ablution area bent over the pool of water, washing his face.

Sani, who always made his ablutions before he left home, took off his slippers at the bottom step of the main stairs, crossed the five-foot corridor where the man was sleeping, and went into the main prayer hall. The imam was sweeping the carpet, and Zul and Sahak were laying and straightening the prayer mats. These were, among others, Sani's main chore every morning. He felt guilty. He wanted to ask about the intruder, and about the man he saw at the ablution area, but the bilal's sweet voice was ringing around the prayer hall and echoing all over the village.

Then he felt a hand touching his shoulder softly. He turned around and saw the man who he deduced had been sleeping outside. The moment Sani saw his face, Sani froze. The man extended his hand to shake Sani's, but Sani just stared at him.

"Assalamu'alaikum," the man greeted Sani.

"Wa alaikum salam," Sani answered softly. He took the man's hand with both his hands and squeezed it firmly. He looked into the man's eyes, and the man nodded his head. Sani collapsed.

Sani missed his dawn prayer. The imam had him put in his room-cum-office with the help of the stranger, Sahak, Zul, and two other patrons who just happened to arrive at the time Sani keeled over. It was a good thing that the stranger was holding his hand as he fell limp. Otherwise, he would have fallen backwards and probably hit his head against the base of one of the concrete pillars that lined the mosque on both sides of the prayer hall.

Sani sat up on the sofa he had been laid upon. It was bright outside. The clock on one of the walls showed about a quarter past eight.

Sani looked around the room. He realized that he had never been in this room before. Although his main responsibility was the upkeep and maintenance of the mosque, the Imam had never asked him into his office. It was an oblong room about three metres wide and maybe five metres long. The sofa Sani had been lying on was right in the centre of the room, facing the Imam's desk. The desk reminded Sani of the teacher's desk in a classroom. Behind the desk, Sani saw the back of a patent leather swivel chair; and behind the chair was a whiteboard with the schedule of lectures and the invited religious teachers who would give them for the current month. Sani saw the imam's name was listed for most of the days. He was, after all, a retired headmaster of a nearby religious school. On the left corner, from Sani's point of view, was a beige steel filing cabinets; in the other corner was a grey, ancient-looking safe in which, Sani presumed, the collections from the patrons of the mosque were kept before they were deposited into the mosque's current account with one of the local banks in town.

"Assalamualaikum, how are you, Sani?" asked the imam as he entered the room, with the stranger following behind him.

"Wa'alaikum salam, Imam. I don't feel too good. Can I take the day off, Imam?"

"Of course, take a rest. Maybe you've been working too hard." The imam was sympathetic. "This is Encik Mustafa. He's from Naratiwat – a businessman. His van broke down just a mile or so from here last night. That's how he ended up at our mosque. Have you arranged for somebody to fix the van, Encik Mustafa?" the imam said, getting Sani up to speed.

"Oh yes, Imam. Thank you very much. The young man – er, Zul and I – we managed to find a mechanic with a tow truck, and he's taken it to their workshop. Still, I need to deliver the package in the van to Singapore, so my company is sending down another van. They'll arrive tonight. In the meantime, I would like to ask your permission, Imam, to stay here for the day until the van arrives," Mustafa said.

"En. Mustafa, why don't you stay at my house? I am staying alone. There's a bedroom you can use and a proper bathroom for you to freshen up," Sani offered hospitality.

"Yes, good idea, Sani," the imam agreed.

"Thank you very much, Encik Sani," Mustafa said.

Sani got up from the sofa and suddenly felt his knees buckle. By reflex, he grabbed Mustafa's arm. He managed to steady himself and gave a wry smile.

"Come, Encik Sani, let me walk you home," Mustafa volunteered.

"Thank you," Sani said.

The imam smiled at both of them. As he held the door open for them, the good imam couldn't help but notice how much Sani and Mustafa resembled each other; but he never thought more of it.

Later that day, just before dusk, as the imam and the bilal were preparing for the dusk prayer and the night's scheduled sermon, a van came into the village. The driver stopped by the mosque to ask if Encik Mustafa was there. The bilal showed him the way to Sani's house.

At prayer time, Encik Mustafa came by the mosque to join the prayer and sat in to listen to the imam's sermon before he got on his way to deliver his package to Singapore. He wanted to properly say thanks to the imam and the bilal and also to Sani. Also, this would give time for his driver to take a rest. Sani was still feeling under the weather and did not join the night's congregation.

Midway through the imam's sermon, the van driver came running into the mosque. He whispered something into the ear of Encik Mustafa, who in turn went up to the imam and whispered the same to him.

The imam had a puzzled look on his face, but he made an announcement that the evening's sermon had to be cut short because something had happened to Sani. The imam, the bilal, and the whole congregation of about twenty men and five women got up and followed the imam to Sani's house.

The house was rather dark. The driver said that Sani wasn't feeling well and asked him to turn off most of the lights, as they were giving him a headache. The driver switched off all the lights except the one in the living room, where he laid himself down on the floor to take a nap before continuing the journey to Singapore with his boss. He was just about to doze off when he heard Sani gave out a moan and then become quiet. He called out to Sani, but no answer came. He approached Sani, who was lying flat on his back on his bed, and shook his shoulder gently, but Sani was unresponsive.

Worried, he ran to the mosque. He was a bit hesitant to enter, being a non-Muslim, but managed to see Encik Mustafa. He took off his slippers and traipsed gently between the men sitting in lotus position. Some stared intently at him, an obvious non-Muslim with his tattooed forearm, in a Muslim house of prayer.

When the imam got to Sani's bedroom, he ordered for the lights to be turned on. Once the room was fully lighted, the imam, the bilal, and the people of the congregation who were crowding the bedroom door let out a gasp. The body lying on the bed was that of an old man. The imam asked for forgiveness from Allah.

"Imam, what happed to Sani?" asked Sahak, who was among the first to come to Sani's side.

"Allah only knows, Sahak. But I believe he is now his real age. Somehow, his real age caught up with him. Such is the will of Allah," the imam told Sahak and the people. "Please do not shame the dead. We must bear only good thoughts of Sani. Keep this among us and within this village."

The villagers in the house, jostling and stretching their necks to see, all agreed with the imam.

"Let us prepare Sani for his final resting place," the imam said.

Encik Mustafa, his eyes watery, insisted that he would help to carry the body to the mosque to be bathed, cleansed, and shrouded. Sani's body was laid to rest that very night, buried next to his mother.

Mustafa took his leave, thanking the imam and the villagers for their hospitality. He and the driver drove off into the night.

"How's Mak?" someone in the back of the van asked.

"She's fine and sends her regards. Abah has been sick along time. She's sad but relieved that his suffering is over. But she is still quite angry about us doing this. She didn't cry when Abah died. She was by his side all the way. But she cried when we took him out of the hospital and into the van to take him here. She just gave Abah a kiss on the forehead and turned away," Mustafa said.

"But this what Abah wanted. He asked for this specifically. And it was his last wish," Sani said.

"Yes, she knew that. That's why she didn't say anything. But you know how we are supposed to treat the dead with the highest respect. We must bathe and cleanse and pray for them and then bury them as soon as possible. That's the Muslim way. We've asked a few ustaz about this, and they say we must also respect his last wish. But we have to do this quickly," Mustafa explained. There were tears in his eyes.

"By the way the buckling knees as you got up were a nice touch." Mustafa smiled.

"Hahaha, yes. It just came to me there and then. It will be helpful when you find me dead tonight," Sani said.

"And the collapsing this morning? That came to you just then too?" Mustafa asked.

"No, that was real. Maybe I thought you wouldn't come here for another week," Sani said.

****

Two years earlier, when he was diagnosed with stage four lung cancer, Ma Lai Long told his family that he would like for his final resting place to be in the village where he was born.

Many decades earlier, when he was twenty-eight years old, Ma Lai Long fled to neighbouring Thailand in a desperate attempt to escape from the British-controlled authorities who were hunting down members of the Communist Party of Malaya. Henceforth, he never returned to his homeland, not by choice but because he was labelled as a known terrorist and was responsible for the deaths of at least one British planter.

Ma Lai Long was not Chinese. He was a Malay Muslim man who was taken in by the ideology of common ownership of communism. Perhaps, motivated by the fact that his beautiful sister was forced to be a consort to the sultan, he wished for a world without castes. His real name was Ahmad Sani bin Suandi.

Originally from Muar, Johor, Ahmad Sani went to Sitiawan, Perak, to find a job. He was a graduate of a teachers college up north, and one of his friends had written to him that there was a job opening in Sitiawan for a translator in a foreign-owned power plant company.

Shortly after he started working, he became very active in the trade union movements. He rose in the ranks of the trade union quickly and caught the attention of the local Communist Party leader. Soon, he became a member of the Communist Party of Malaya. This was before the party was declared illegal following the assassination of three British planters in Perak. Ahmad Sani, though he was never actively involved, somehow found himself in the thick of the conflict and was, under unfortunate circumstances, named as one of the men wanted by the British authorities. His real name was never revealed, either intentionally by the authorities or because they do not know who he really was. He was identified by the nickname given by the Communist Party leader who recruited him, 'Malay Dragon'. He found himself running into the jungles of Perak together with a regiment of the Communist Party and managed to cross the Thai border, out of the jurisdiction of the British authorities.

His parents did not know of his involvement in the Communist Party and were distraught when told by his employers that their son had not reported for work after a few days of absenteeism. Ahmad Sani himself, who could not bear the thought of his family being interrogated, cut all connections to them while on the run by burning all his identification documents. Still, he vowed to one day return to his village.

As far as his family were concerned, Ahmad Sani was a missing person, and within the community of his beloved village, the most popular theory of his disappearance was that he was abducted by the Bunians.

Ahmad Sani married Wan Latifah binti Wan Mokhsen, a Thai woman he met after he settled in a village called Kampung Malaya near the Malaya-Thai border in the Naratiwat province. He changed his name to Abu Bakar bin Abdullah. It was a name he conjured up when he was given a chance to "renew" his Thai identification document. The documents, it was reported, were lost in a fire and were reduced to ashes. Hence he called himself Bakar, which means 'to burn', Abu, which means 'ashes', and Abdullah, which means 'the servant of Allah'. And that he truly became.

He read religious books, sat in religious classes, frequented the village mosque, and totally absorbed himself in his religion. As he grew older, he was accorded the title 'ustaz', which he shunned. But it stuck on him. He had only two children with Latifah, two boys, who grew up to be entrepreneurs in the business of exporting Thai-made goods to Malaysia. Their business thrived, and they frequently plied the north-south highway (and later the expressway) along the west coast of the Malaysia Peninsula. Abu Bakar, as he was thereafter known, named the older boy Ahmad Mustafa and the younger Ahmad Sani, to preserve the name he had been born with.

When their father's condition worsened, the two boys devised a plan to fulfil his final wish. One of Mustafa's and Sani's customers was the art supply shop in Muar. It was from the old, grumpy Chinese shop owner that they learned about the legend of Ahmad Sani, who had disappeared in the jungles of Malaya. The shop owner was, in fact, the man who had recruited Ahmad Sani to join the Communist Party of Malaya. During one of their deliveries, when the old man heard Mustafa calling out to his brother by name, the old man started to tell the story of a man with the same name he had known as a young man in Perak. He laughed out loud when he said that the silly villagers across the river thought the man was abducted by the Bunian people, when he knew for sure that he joined the Communist Party and fled to Thailand. He had kept this to himself all this while to protect himself and his family.

That day, Sani was compelled to tell the old man that he was actually the son of Ma Lai Long. The old man was taken aback. He was surprised that Ma Lai Long was still alive. Sani told him that that would not be the case for long. His father was in the intensive care unit, and the cancer had been detected too late.

The following day, he went back to the art supply shop to seek permission to use their telephone to call his brother and ask of his father's condition. Mustafa told him that his father was not getting better and that the doctors were not optimistic that he would survive the week.

When Mustafa came, Sani knew his father was gone. Mustafa had arranged for his father's body to be transported down to Muar. While his mother – with the help of his trusted workers – went about discharging the body from the hospital and preparing him for the seven-hour trip, Mustafa went ahead to inform his brother.

He reached Muar at around four o'clock in the morning. The broken-down van was a ruse. Parking it by the roadside about a mile from the village, Mustafa cut the fuel hose, draining the van of its petrol. He walked the rest of the distance to the village and lay down to sleep in the mosque's compound. He slept for about an hour or so before he was awoken by the noise just outside the gate. He got up, saw two men in traditional Malay shirt and sarongs with skullcaps on their heads, and presumed that they were the imam and bilal of the mosque. He greeted them from inside the mosque, apologised, and explained about his broken-down van.

The imam and the bilal gave a sigh of relief and opened the gate. The bilal switched on the lights in the mosque and proceed to the azan room for his call of dawn prayers. Sahak and Zul came on their motorcycle asking for the intruder, but the imam calmed them down and introduced them to Mustafa. They too were satisfied with Mustafa's story and proceeded to make ablution. Mustafa asked to use the toilet. Sahak and Zul, after cleansing themselves, helped the imam to lay down the prayer mats, and the imam swept the carpet.

By the time Mustafa went back into the prayer hall, there was another man there. Even from his back, Mustafa knew who he was. He hesitated for a while. He knew his brother would be devastated by the news, but there was no other way to tell him that their father was dead.

Just before dusk, Mustafa's other van came. This was supposedly the replacement van that would help him deliver his goods to their destination while his original transport was being repaired. The van driver, one of Mustafa's staff, stopped by the mosque and asked for Mustafa. The few men there, who had just arrived at the mosque to start the dusk prayer, pointed the driver to Sani's house.

The driver drove to the house and parked as close as possible to the front door. By then, the azan for the dusk prayer was sounding over the loudspeaker atop the minaret next to the mosque. Mustafa went to the mosque to pray. Sani prayed at home and then, with the help of the van driver, brought out his father's remains and placed him carefully on his bed. He kissed his father's cold forehead and then hid in the van.

The driver was sent to the mosque to tell Mustafa the deed was done.

When the driver whispered the message into his ear, Mustafa nodded his head. He sent the driver away. He then went to the front of the mosque, where the imam was giving a sermon from a book, and told the imam that something has happened to Sani and he might be dead. The whole congregation left the mosque, and as the word spread, it looked like everyone in the village was heading toward Sani's house.

The imam was the first to Sani's deathbed, and he got an even bigger shock to find an old man's body in it. The imam looked closely at the deceased and saw the strong resemblance to Sani. *Of course,* deduced the imam, *Sani is now showing his true age.* He uttered praises to Allah and asked for his forgiveness. The whole village wanted to see Sani even more when the whispers spread that Sani had died and his age had caught up to him. Sahak and Zul told of how Sani had suddenly collapsed in the mosque just before the dawn prayer and that there were signs of him having the premonition of his own death.

Sani senior's body was properly bathed and cleansed and was brought to the mosque to be prayed for. That very night, the villagers sent him to the nearby Muslim cemetery, where he was given the proper burial that he wished for. Sani junior, all this while, had to stay quietly in the van.

He took some time to stay by his father. He asked his forgiveness and prayed that Allah would forgive him, his father, and Mustafa. He wanted to have more time, but the driver was getting fidgety.

These villagers, had they known that his father had joined the Communist Party, would not have accepted his father's wish to be buried here. But Ahmad Sani bin Suandi fulfilled both his vows, to return home and to be buried in the place he was born.

Oil from a Murdered Man's Chin

Awang had once been in the army, spending most of his career guarding the Malaysia-Thai border. After his retirement, at the age of forty-five, he came back to the village where he grew up and settled down in his old, dilapidated abandoned family house. He had not been to this village for a few decades, and so he hardly knew these villagers, nor did the villagers recognise him as the young adult who left this village to join the army a long, long time ago. In the first few months after his return, he stayed indoors most of the time, cleaning up the old house and making repairs. He came out only to get provisions for his sustenance once a week and his pension from the town post office once a month.

Awang was the youngest of three siblings. This house, the very house he was born in, had been empty since he joined the army at age eighteen. His mother died a long time ago when was young. His father, also dead by the time he was discharged, had remarried, and his two sisters (he was the only boy in the family) followed their respective husbands to live in the city. At some point, they had all moved away to start their own separate lives.

Imam Sabri, the local cleric, noticed Awang ambling in front of the mosque one day on his way to town. He thought Awang looked familiar and decided to give him a visit that night, after the night prayer. Sure enough, as the imam interviewed Awang, he found out that Awang was the only son of his friend Abdul Kulop, who had remarried a divorcée a few months after his wife died and moved away from this village. Abdul Kulop, Awang said, had died last year of a heart attack. He was seventy-one years old. Awang did not go the funeral, as his stepmother, stepsiblings, and even his own sisters forgot to convey the news of his father's death to him. He only knew that his father had died in a letter his eldest sister sent him a month later.

Imam Sabri kept visiting Awang almost daily. At first Awang found this annoying. Gradually the imam managed to coax Awang to join the occasional congregations at the mosque.

After a while, Awang became a regular at the mosque, although he still kept to himself and only talked to Imam Sabri. He would be among the first ones to arrive at the mosque before every prayer time, but instead of mingling with the other patrons, he would find a secluded corner and start reading the Qur'an softly as he waited for the azan.

Other than that, his daily routine would be spent repairing and fixing the old house. And he liked this new existence, living in his own place and at his own pace. During his time in the army, he had felt he was always taking orders and constantly watched.

One day a villager was taken ill with a high fever and was bleeding from his mouth, ears, and nose. He complained of joint pains, and rashes appeared on his body, but he refused to be taken to hospital for fear of being detained. And besides, he was convinced that he was the victim of black magic, administered by someone who was jealous of him winning the consolation prize in the last four-digit lottery draw, the first time he had ever won after almost thirty years of betting.

A fellow villager ran over to the mosque seeking help from the imam. It was late in the night, and coincidently, Awang was just closing up the mosque after everybody else had gone. The imam had been away for that day and the following day, attending a seminar for imams in Kuala Lumpur. The bilal, considered second in command, had gone off right after the end of the night prayer, having promised a relative who lived in another village thirty kilometres away that he would help in the preparation of the relative's daughter's wedding the next day. So, the bilal delegated the task of closing up the mosque to Awang.

And being considered a pious person by his association to the mosque, the distressed villager called upon him to help. He refused at first, but when promised that he would be paid, he agreed to take a look at the ailing man.

After satisfying himself that the mosque was secured, he followed his caller to the house of the sick man. He was shown to the man's bedside and given a plastic chair to sit on near the head of the man. The poor man was lying on his back, shivering, with traces of red at the corners of his mouth. For a few moments, Awang just sat there, looking at the man from head to toe, not really knowing what to do.

"How is he?" somebody asked Awang.

"Why was he not sent to the hospital?" Awang asked. He touched the man's forehead with the back of his hand. It was very hot.

"This is black magic, Awang. Sending him to the hospital won't help him. Somebody did this to him, Awang. Do you know who?" the same person asked again.

Awang turn his head slightly in the direction of the person. "No," Awang said in a low, steady tone. He felt disgusted that in this day and age, these people were still so backward that they believed in black magic. He stared at the shivering man for a while and then said softly, "It's too late. I cannot save him. He will die tomorrow."

Then he got up and left. He had seen the same thing before. One of his fellow soldiers had taken ill and had the same symptoms. It was Leptospirosis, or rat's urine disease.

Somewhere in the house, as he walked briskly back to his house, Awang heard the wailing of a woman, presumably the dying man's wife.

The man died the next day, and Awang's powers of prediction were held in awe by the villagers. After the funeral, the widow came to see Awang and asked him to protect her and her children. Awang told her it was the work of Allah and she must seek His help. She insisted that Awang gave her something. Awang was exasperated, and just to be rid of her, he told the grieving widow to purchase a pouch of frankincense. She did, and she came back and gave it to Awang, expecting him to read a mantra over it. Again, wanting to get her away from his house, he read one or two verses from the Quran that he knew over the pouch and gave it to her. She gave him RM50. He refused, she insisted, and he relented.

Thereafter, Awang was accorded by the villagers the title Bomoh (shaman). He did not like this new status. His once-tranquil life was consistently interrupted by villagers with the strangest requests and at the oddest hours. The villagers would come to his house to get a pouch of frankincense for one thing or another. Some asked if he could give them the winning numbers for the next four-digit draw, some asked for a pouch of frankincense to bring more customers to their shop, some wanted a pouch to help their children with their school exams, some asked to ward off evil spirits, and some wanted to help their daughters find a husband.

Awang had never been a confrontational character, and when these people insisted that he give them a pouch of frankincense, he obliged simply to be rid of them as quickly as possible. They offered him payments in return, but he refused. The villagers then hung an empty powdered milk can with a slit cut on its lid just outside his door, and they would put in money after Awang had given them a pouch.

In the week after the man died and he was made a Bomoh by the villagers, he had no less than ten 'consultations'. Although he saw the tin can hanging on the wall every time he walked in and out of the kitchen door, he never really gave it much thought. He did not believe anybody would actually put money in it.

But one afternoon, after a rather heavy rain, Awang noted that the tin had come off the nail that held it against the wooden wall and rolled under his house. The lid had come off, and he saw currency notes strewn along the path. He collected the money, most of it drenched with rain water, and retrieved the tin can. Inside the can, Awang was surprised to see more money. The rain had seeped through the slit on the lid and filled the can halfway until the nail that was holding it up could no longer stand the weight. He poured out the remaining water in the tin, collected the notes that were on the ground, and brought them into his kitchen.

He took out all the money from the can carefully, as the notes were wet and would easily tear. He put a large serving tray over his cooking hob, turned on the fire, and spread out each note. Most of them were five-ringgit and ten-ringgit notes. He counted them and found he had made RM250 from his ten consultations.

This is good business! He thought to himself. If he could make RM250 in a week, he could easily rake in RM1,000 a month. This was more than enough for his sustenance. And best of all, he would no longer need to walk out to the main street, wait indefinitely for a bus, walk again to the post office, wait in line to take his pension out, and repeat the process in reverse on his way back home.

"Awang!" someone called out to him from outside as he was picking up the dried notes from the tray. "Awang! Are you home?"

"Yes! Yes!" Awang answered as he looked around to find a place to put away the money. He saw a plastic container which he used to hold biscuits. He poured out whatever was in the container onto a dining plate, blew out the tiny bits of crumbs remaining, put the money in, and snapped the cover on.

Awang opened the kitchen door and called out to his visitor. There were loose planks and termite-infested beams that he was replacing in the front part of the house, so he had been receiving his visitors in the kitchen since the day he returned home.

His caller walked around to the back, and Awang saw it was Atan. Atan had come last week asking for the winning four-digit number. This worried Awang a little. Maybe Atan wanted his money back or, worse, planned to beat him up for giving the wrong number.

"Awang!" Atan greeted him with a grin. "Thank you, thank you." Atan took Awang's right hand with both hands and shook it vigorously. "I won the consolation prize. I bet ten ringgit, and I won RM1,000. Thank you, thank you," Atan said.

When Awang pulled his hand away, in it was a fifty-ringgit note.

"Just a token," Atan said when he saw Awang's surprised expression. Atan turned around and walked to his home, which Awang only then realised was a mere ten metres away. Atan gave Awang a final wave before going up the steps into his house.

*****

The next morning, when the dawn prayers were done, Imam Sabri scanned the attendance and could not see Awang. He delegated down to the bilal to read out the morning sermon, as he was very concerned about Awang, who almost never missed the dawn prayer.

He called out and knocked on Awang's kitchen door, knowing that Awang was living in the kitchen until he finished repairing the front living area of his house.

"Awang! Awang! It's me, the imam. Are you all right?" the imam shouted. Something stirred within Awang's house, and then the imam heard the clacking of latches before the kitchen door was opened. Awang stood there, still half asleep.

"Why didn't you come for the dawn prayer? Are you all right? Are you sick?" the imam asked.

"Sorry, Imam. I had a few things to do. I only went to sleep at about four this morning," Awang said.

"What were you doing?" the imam was curious.

"Err, something." Awang suddenly stopped himself from divulging too much of his activities the night before.

"Why is your kitchen smoky and smelling of incense?" the imam asked.

"Nothing, Imam. It's nothing. Err … I am sorry I missed the dawn prayer. I promise to be there for the dzuhur prayer," Awang answered quickly.

The imam looked at him with suspicion. "All right, I will see you at the mosque," he said and walked off.

But Awang did not turn up as promised. After the imam left, he thought he needed just a few more minutes of sleep and lay down on his bed. He fell asleep and only woke up at two in the afternoon.

The night before, at about ten, Awang had received another visitor. Just as he was preparing for bed, Awang heard soft knocking sounds on his kitchen door. For a while he thought it was just the wind or a gecko knocking its tail against the wall. It was only when the knocking came at a constant rhythm that Awang decided to investigate and opened the door. He got a shock to find a woman standing outside his door. He could not see her face, as she held a sarong over her head so that the upper part of her face was in darkness.

"Assalamualaikum, Pak Awang," she said, almost in a whisper.

Awang did not answer. He wasn't sure that she was human.

175

"Who are you? What are you doing at my house in the middle of the night?" Awang said boldly, but his heart was racing. *This must be a ghost,* he thought.

"It's me. The wife of Mat Dan," the woman said.

"Mat Dan?" Awang did not know anyone by that name.

"Yes, Mat Dan who died a few days ago," the woman tried to explain. "Our house is over there. You came to see him, but you said you could not save him."

"Ohh …" Awang remembered. It was the man who died of rat urine disease. Awang wanted to say this, but instead he said, "The man who died of black magic?"

The woman gave out a little cry and nodded her head.

Awang waited in silence for the woman to regain her composure. When she did, she said to Awang, "I want you to avenge his death. Do to whoever did that to him, exactly what was did to him."

"No, I don't think that would be a good idea," Awang said. *And I don't know how,* he continued his sentence in his head.

The woman sobbed again. Awang was getting uncomfortable having a whispering conversation at night with a widow of a recently deceased man. "OK, OK," Awang said. "I'll see what I can do."

"Thank you, Pak Awang, thank you," she said with a little smile on her lips. Awang still could not see the rest of her face. "Here," she said, giving Awang an envelope.

"What's this?" Awang asked. He looked at the envelope but did not take it.

"Just a token," she said, holding out the envelope to Awang.

"No need for that," Awang said.

She kept holding out the envelope until Awang felt he had no choice but to accept it. The moment Awang took the envelope, she turned around and walked briskly back home. Awang closed the kitchen door and locked it. He looked inside the envelope to find two fifty-ringgit notes. Feeling obligated, Awang decided he should earn the money. So he burnt some frankincense in an antique brass urn and started to recite whatever verses from the Quran he could remember (which were just the ones he and every Muslim learned as a child). He must have fallen asleep while reciting the verses and sitting in a lotus position on the kitchen floor. He had a dream that his mother was alive and the house was as he remembered it while he grew up. There were many people there, none of whom he recognised. It was a celebration of something, and everyone was in a jovial mood. Then his mother asked Awang to follow her. Something reminded him that if you follow a dead person, then you will die too. He refused. His mother begged him to come with her, but he kept saying no to her and started to cry. He wanted to be with her, but he was not ready to die. Then Awang felt a sharp pin on his chest, and he was back in the kitchen. He was lying flat on his back on the cold cement floor of the kitchen. His chest was hurting. The kitchen was full of smoke from the burning incense. He got up, drizzled some water in the incense burning bowl to put out the smouldering amber, and lay down on his mattress. But he tossed and turned, only falling asleep when it almost dawn and awakening when he heard the imam call his name the next morning.

*****

After the dusk prayer, Imam Sabri went to look for Awang. He had not turned up at the mosque as he had promised. In fact, Awang had missed all the day's prayers at the mosque. The imam was very concerned. The smell of incense in Awang's house that morning made him think that Awang might have become deviant. He had heard lately that Awang was referred to as Bomoh by the villagers after the death of Mat Dan. Awang had told the imam that it was really rat's urine disease, and they both uttered their disappointment with the villagers' ignorance. They both laughed at Awang's bomoh status and brushed it off to be a fleeting thing.

But as he approached Awang's house, he knew what he feared was really happening. There were people outside his house, waiting in line to have a session with Bomoh Awang.

"What are you all doing here?" asked the imam, his brows furrowed. He looked at each one of the villagers, who were either sitting on various objects outside Awang's kitchen or just standing around, talking to each other.

"We are waiting our turn to see Awang, Pak Imam," answered one villager, who was leaning against the wall next to the closed kitchen door. "But you can go in before us. We don't mind," said the man, grinning. The rest of the people there, mostly men, agreed. They nodded their heads and smiled at the imam as he look at them one by one.

"Yes, I do want to see him," the imam said and proceeded to open the door. But the man leaning there stopped him.

"Pak Imam, there is someone inside. Let the lady finish her session," the man said, still smiling.

"Lady? Awang is in there with a woman?" The imam sounded alarmed.

"Yes, Pak Imam. Don't worry, Pak Awang is a good man. He won't do anything ... er ... to her," said the man.

"Pak Imam, have a seat," said another man there, putting a weathered plastic chair near the imam.

The imam shook his head. He didn't want to soil his white tunic.

Then the door opened and smoke billowed out. The woman, the imam recognised, was the widow of Mat Dan.

"Hey, Senah, what are you doing here?" the imam called out as the woman went past him. She was a little shocked to see him there. The imam scolded her for wailing her lungs out at her husband's funeral. When she said her husband was a victim of black magic, the imam scolded her some more, saying that believing in other powers beside Allah was an unforgivable sin.

"Nothing, Pak Imam," was her reply. She quickly took her leave.

The imam shook his head and went inside. Awang too was surprised to see the imam. He did not think the imam would actually be looking for him at his house at night. The kitchen reeked of frankincense and was filled with smoke rising from a brass incense bowl. The air was stifling due to the heat from the glowing embers in the incense bowl. Awang was on the floor, sitting before the incense bowl. There were other things in front of him: a small metal basin filled with water, some betel leaves, betel nut, one young coconut, and some lime in another bowl, together with a huge army knife presumably used to cut the lime. Strewn outside the same bowl were squeezed-out lime quarters.

"What is all this, Awang? This is Syirik! You must stop this nonsense!" Imam Sabri almost shouted.

Awang was taken aback by the imam's outburst. He in all honesty and, perhaps, naivety, did not expect the imam would be so angry and accuse him of worshipping other than Allah.

"But, Pak Imam, I have the gift." The words spurted out of his mouth before he could stop himself.

"What are you talking about? What gift?" The imam was losing his temper.

"Err ... I can predict the future, and I can turn black magic back unto those who cast it," Awang said.

"What?" The imam felt he should give Awang a slap.

"Mat Dan, who died last week – someone cast a spell on him. I returned the spell, and yesterday, the culprit who sent it to him died. Didn't you hear, Pak Imam? Usop Semaon died this morning in the same way as Mat Dan did. Mat Dan's widow just came to confirm that Usop and Mat Dan were each supposed to give RM500 to bet on last month's four-digit draw. But Usop could not fork out the money, so Mat Dan went in alone. He pawned his wife's gold and managed to get the whole RM1,000. When Usop heard Mat Dan won RM100,000, Usop came for his share. Usop said he was the one who got the number from some grave-worshipping ritual. Mat Dan said he was the one who put in all the money, and he brushed Usop off by giving him a token of RM100. When Mat Dan's widow asked if I could find out who cast the bad spell on her late husband, I said I would try. And the next day, Usop died the same way as Mat Dan did," Awang explained to Imam Sabri. He was still sitting on the floor. He told the story in a monotonous voice, as if to say he should be accredited for the death of Usop Semaon.

The imam looked around for a place to sit. He pulled a wooden chair that was tucked under an ancient-looking wooden table with a plastic floral-patterned tablecloth. "Are you serious, Awang? You knew what actually killed Mat Dan; you told me that. And Usop probably died of the same thing. Those two were best friends. They went everywhere together, fishing, hunting, and whatever else." The imam was shaking his head in disbelief.

Awang did not move from his lotus position on the floor. There was silence for a while before Awang said in a low, growling voice, "Are you denying the powers bestowed upon me by God? You, a man of God, deny the very sign that God has shown you? You disbelieve that the things that happened were the will of God and that they happened through my action? Do you still deny I am the *chosen one?*"

Awang's voice rose until he was shouting at the top of his lungs. It frightened Imam Sabri. Awang had gone mad. With the only exit being the door he came in through and the army knife beside Awang, he knew he must leave the smoky kitchen immediately. He gathered his tunic in a bunch with one hand, slowly lifted himself up off the old wooden chair with the other, and made a dash for the door. He pulled hard on the huge rusty latch. It opened, but he had pulled too quickly, and the bottom of the door hit his bare big toe. It stung and made him let go of the latch. The door bounced off his big toe and slammed shut. Looking down, he saw blood oozing from under the nail of his big toe. Then he saw from the corner of his eyes that Awang was reaching for the knife, though he had not budged from his sitting position. The poor imam panicked, screamed out loud "Allahuakbar!" and pulled the door again, this time making sure his foot was out of the way. He burst out of Awang's kitchen, not bothering to slip on his slippers, and ran barefoot back home as fast as he could.

Awang took a lime from the bowl, put in on the ground, sliced it into four quarters with the huge army knife, and squeezed one quarter into the bowl of water. "Who's next?" he shouted.

The villagers waiting outside were stunned to see the imam running away. It was comical, but it was such a strange sight that they could only stare after the retreating imam with mouths agape.

*****

The next day, Imam Sabri made a police report on Awang's activities. The police took him in for questioning for a day and then released him, since he had not committed any crimes. He did not ask for money, much less extort anyone, and there was no way that Awang could be have been responsible for the death of Mat Dan or Usop. So they let him go. One of the policemen even asked for the winning number from him, and he obliged.

Awang came home in a police car. It was about noon when the police car came into the village, navigating the narrow road. The police car passed the mosque, where, coincidentally, Imam Sabri was dismounting from his motorcycle. Their eyes met. Unseen by the two policemen sitting in front, Awang pointed a warning finger at the imam. Imam stared at Awang until he was out of sight and shook his head.

On their way out, the police were stopped by the imam, who was curious to know why Awang wasn't in jail. The police explained there wasn't any ground for them to put him away. "But he threatened me with a huge knife," Imam Sabri said, unsatisfied with their explanation.

"It's just your word against his. Nobody saw that, and we checked his house. That was the only knife he had, so he used it for to cut everything, even the lime for his readings."

It was the beginning of rivalry between the two men. The imam was not happy with the lack of action on the part of the police. He even complained to the religious authority of the state, but again, they would only recommend consultation for Awang, who, according to them, was yet to commit any blasphemous acts. When Awang's patrons were interviewed, all of them said that Awang only gave them incense and told them to read simple verses from the Quran. Awang always said, according to them, that we should ask for what we want from Allah, for protection and for good fortune. There was nothing deviant about that, the religious authority said. But they did warn Awang not to give out any more winning four-digit draws.

A cycle began. Awang would stop his activities for a few days as directed by the authorities. Then, gradually, he would succumb to the demands of the villagers. His "business" would start to pick up again, and the imam would report him to the authorities. Then he would stop for a few days. Round and round it went for a few months.

Awang did not mind the routine. It brought enough attention to him to generate new business with customers. Whatever collection he made was more than enough for his own sustenance. But as his confidence grew, he felt it was time for him to take a wife. Awang had never married. It was not that he didn't want to, but, spending most of his time in the jungles of Malaya, he did not have many chances to meet women. Besides, he had always been a shy and self-conscious person, and talking to women terrified him. Also, he knew that with his pockmarked face and rather large nose, he was not a handsome man.

One morning, during one of his off periods, Awang decided to go to town. He had not done so for quite some time, and now that he could afford it, he thought maybe he would treat himself to some new clothes. While he was waiting for the bus, a factory bus stopped to drop off a woman. Awang had never seen her before, and he could not help but stare at her. There was something about this woman that attracted him, her height perhaps? She was quite tall, taller than Awang. Her size perhaps? She had a large frame, but she was not fat. Her face? She had dark skin and sharp Indian features. Awang thought she was beautiful.

As she alighted from the bus, their eyes met for a few seconds, and she gave him a smile. He smiled back. His gaze followed her until she turned the corner at the junction of the small village road. He had to know where she lived, so he followed her. To his surprise, she was heading towards his house. She went past it and then into Atan's house. *Oh no, she's Atan's wife.* He gave a sigh and walked the half kilometre back to the bus stop.

Awang spent the day walking around Muar town, shopping and sightseeing. At about noon, he went into a coffee shop to have lunch. The shop belonged to a Chinese man, but he only sold drinks. The food was prepared and sold by a Malay man. There were satay and various types of rice and noodle dishes.

"Hey, Awang! What are you doing here?" Atan greeted Awang as he was searching for a place to sit in the crowded little shop. Atan was standing behind him and seemed to have appeared out of nowhere.

"Oh, Atan. I was just looking for a few things," Awang said. "And you?"

"I work here," Atan said in a cheery voice. "Come, I am on my lunch break. We can sit over there." Atan ushered Awang to a table placed against the back wall. On it was a bunch of vegetable in a plastic basket. Atan sent the vegetables to the kitchen, came back a few moments later with a smelly damp cloth, and wiped everything that was on the table, mostly bits of vegetables, onto the floor.

"What do want to eat?" Atan asked Awang. "Our specialty is *Mee Bandung,*" he continued, grinning at Awang.

"OK, I'll have that and iced tea, please," Awang replied. Atan zipped to the kitchen, shouted Awang's order at the cook, and then shouted to the Chinese man at the counter, "One iced tea please, Towkay!"

Then Atan sat with Awang. "Pak Awang," Atan said in a lowered tone. Awang could not be more than a few years older than Atan. But ever since Awang had acquired shaman status, Atan, like everyone else, had been addressing him with the avuncular title "Pak."

"I need your help. It's about my daughter. She's seeing this Bangla. I don't like it. I think he's just trying to get a citizenship by marrying her," Atan confided in Awang.

Awang's order came just as he was about to ask Atan something. He waited until the food and drink were put on the table and the waiter went away before asking, "What can I do?"

"I am sure the Bangla has put a spell on her," Atan said. "That's why she wants him. He's married, you know. He has a wife waiting for him in Bangladesh, and he's gallivanting with my daughter here."

"How do you know he's married?" Awang asked, wiping his mouth with a white serviette.

"Oh, I heard from the Bangla's housemate," Atan said.

"Hmm." Awang nodded. "But I still don't know what you expect me to do."

"I want you to break the spell. Get my daughter to come to her senses and see that the Bangla is just using her."

By this time, Awang had finished his *Mee Bandung* and was sipping his iced tea through a transparent plastic straw.

"But what if your daughter is really in love with him? What if she doesn't care if he's married or just using her to get citizenship?" Awang laid out the scenarios.

"Pak Awang, I am a widower ... well, not really. My wife is crazy. She's in a crazy house somewhere. I can't work. I am not well. This job is just temporary. I am doing it because I owe the towkay some money. I don't want the Bangla to take my daughter away. I ... I love her too much," Atan said, trying to sound sad and hoping some tears would well up in his eyes.

"Your wife is ... not living with you?" Awang heart jumped. The woman he had seen must have been Atan's daughter.

"No, just me and my daughter ... my stepdaughter, actually," Atan said.

"Wei! Atan, you want to work or you want to talk with your friend?" the Chinese man behind the counter at the front of the shop shouted.

"I am on my break, towkay, relax laa," Atan shouted back.

"How many breaks you want to take? Get back to work!" the towkay replied.

"OK! OK!" Atan shouted back. And to Awang he said, "I see you tonight, OK?"

"OK," Awang said. "But I'll come to your house."

That night, after dusk, Awang went to Atan's house, not fifty metres away from his own home. He called out to Atan, who almost immediately opened the door.

"Awang, come, come. My daughter just left. We can talk freely about what to do to her so she will forget the Bangla." Atan beckoned Awang up to his living room.

"She's not home? Did she go off to work already? She works at the factory, right? I saw her getting off the factory bus this morning," Awang said, disappointed.

"No, she's on leave today. She said she's going out to town with a few friends. But I know she went out with that Bangla. We must stop this, Pak Awang, please," Atan begged.

Awang could see what a lazy bum Atan was. Awang had asked one of his regular customers about Atan and learned that Atan was not native to this village. He had moved here from another village further south. Not many people knew about his background because he did not really get along well with people. He had a temper and was especially sensitive about people asking him what he did for a living.

The villagers concluded that Atan was a lazy bum who lived off his stepdaughter. His wife, rumours had it, had gone mad after she found him cheating on her. She tried to kill herself but failed and became a permanent resident of the psychiatric ward at the Muar General Hospital.

"Maybe I can help you, Atan. But this time I will have to ask for a price," Awang said seriously. They were sitting in the living area of Atan's house on cushions over a wooden settee. Atan made hot tea, but Awang took one sip and found it overly sweet.

"Whatever you want that I have is yours," Atan said.

Awang thought for a while about what he was about to say. Would Atan be angry? Would Atan attack him physically? Or would Atan accept him as his son-in-law?

"I want your stepdaughter," Awang said, in a steady, monotonous voice.

"What?" Atan said, although he had heard clearly the words from Awang's mouth.

"I want to marry her, make her my wife," Awang continued in his monotonous voice. There was not to be a negotiation, he seemed to imply. It was either him or the Bangla.

Atan looked at Awang's face to see if he would crack a smile and say that he was just joking. But nothing came from Awang.

"You are serious," Atan said.

"I am serious. I can take care of her. She will be here, not far from you. I have my army pension and the contributions from the villagers. And you don't have to find work. I will have enough to take care of both of you," Awang said, still maintaining his business-like tone.

Atan thought about all Awang had said. It sounded good. *I don't have to work, and my son-in-law can predict 4D numbers. I don't have to worry about Sue ... Not a bad deal.*

"OK, I agree. She is yours," Atan said. "But what will you do about the Bangla?"

"I have looked in the bowl," Awang said, referring to the bowl of water he used to tell fortunes. "And I see that she is a victim of black magic. The foreigner, he has used the oil from a murdered man's chin on her. Do you know of this oil?"

"Yes, of course. I thought this was just an old wives' tale." Atan was amazed.

"Well, when I was patrolling the Thai border, I once met an old man who actually made the oil. I don't know his race or religion, but I met him in the jungle. I remember, I had a stomach ache and had to 'go'. I was doing my business when I smelled something burning. It was like a barbecue. I was hungry, and the smell reminded me of satay. I followed my nose, and it brought me to a clearing. There was this old man sitting in front of something that was giving out a flickering light. I thought it was some kind of lamp, but he was looking at it intently and occasionally, bending forward to add or remove something from whatever was giving out the light.

"I came out in to the clearing and startled the old man. He wanted to run away, but whatever was burning there was too precious to be left. He said something in Thai, raising his hand in surrender. I pointed my gun at him and approached the source of light. It was a small contraption. There was a small fire. Over it was a receptacle collecting a liquid that was dripping from a severed head hanging on a frame made of tree branches. The heat from the fire was melting the rotting flesh of the human head. The dripping oil was captured by the metal receptacle, which funnelled it into little bottles with 'essence of vanilla' labels on them."

Atan listened to Awang's story in awe. "What did you do? Did you get some of the oil?"

"No. I thought it was disgusting that you need to use black magic to make someone like or love you," Awang said. "So I killed the old man and burnt his contraption and the severed head."

"You could have made a lot of money ..." Atan sighed.

"Well, your daughter is a victim. How do you feel about that?" Awang retorted.

"How can you break the spell?" Atan asked.

"Before I shot him dead, the old man said that once the oil is applied to someone, the only way to break the spell is to kill the person who applied it," Awang said.

"Really? I've never heard that." Atan was not agreeable with the idea of murder. "I don't think we should kill him. Can't we just scare him off?"

"Scare him off? Of course we can, but the next day your daughter will be gone too. He'll find a way to contact her. We need to make him disappear, to not exist anymore. Only then the spell will be broken," Awang argued.

Atan thought that made good sense. "What about the police?"

"What about them? If we hide the body well, nobody will ever find him. We can even bury him in the old cemetery. Who goes there anyway? So what if he doesn't report for work? Do you think the factory owners will make a missing person report? These workers are illegal. The factory can't take the chance. They'll just hire another worker. His fellow workers? Are they going to the police? They are the ones who will be jailed." Awang gave out a little laugh, which sounded more like he was trying to clear his nose.

"How are we going to do this?" asked Atan after a long pause. Awang made a lot of sense as far as he was concerned.

"We'll have to do it tonight. You wait for them to come back from their date. Then you tell your daughter to go home. You get the foreigner to come with you to the old cemetery. I will wait there." Awang paused for a while to think. "I think I will need help. Is there anyone we can trust? Someone not too clever who is willing to make some money, no questions asked?"

"Why?" Atan wondered.

"I don't think I can carry him alone. Also, I will need help to dig a grave to bury him," Awang said.

"How about Udin?" suggested Atan.

"Who is Udin?"

"He's a homeless man. He likes to hang around this village in the evening because the villagers here give him food. He wanders around in Muar town the whole day, asking people for money. Then he walks back all the way here and sleeps wherever he can, usually at the bus stop, unless it rained. Then he'll sleep under somebody's house. He'll do anything you ask, if you promise to give him money. He's probably at the bus stop by now," Atan said, looking at the clock on his wall.

"Hmm … he will be perfect. What time do you think will your daughter be back?" Awang asked.

"I told her to be back by ten, but probably she'll stay out till midnight."

"OK. At ten we find Udin and bring him to the old cemetery. He and I will dig a grave for the foreigner. You wait somewhere between the cemetery and your house, somewhere they will surely pass by. Then you challenge him to a duel. He will have to accept if he has any honour in him. Ask him to get in your car and say the duel will take place in the old cemetery. As soon as he gets out of your car, you drive home and make sure your daughter does not go out. If she knows what has happened to her boyfriend, she may go mad." Awang had been thinking out this plan ever since his meeting with Atan at the coffee shop in Muar town. Atan's daughter would be his wife. "What is your daughter's name?"

Atan was listening intently to Awang's plan. It sounded plausible, and he would not be involved in the murder. He would just drop the foreign worker off at the cemetery.

"Sudarseh. I call her Sue," Atan answered.

*****

Atan drove his old, rusty car to the bus top. There he saw Udin. He was straddling the cement bench at the bus stop and having his dinner out of a brown wrapping paper. Atan parked his car a little way from the bus stop and walked back towards Udin, who was oblivious of anything going on around him; his full focus was on the rice and curry in front of him.

"Oi, Udin," Atan called out as he approached the hunched figure in the semidarkness, lighted by the dim fluorescence under the roof of the bus stop.

Udin looked up, lifted his chin to acknowledge the existence of Atan, and continued eating. He was eating with his hands, and Atan wondered where, when, and how he washed them.

"Udin, how would you like to make some money?" Atan asked, sitting in front of Udin with Udin's dinner in between them. Udin probably had not bathed for a long time. His body odour mingled with the smell of curry and occasional diesel from a passing vehicle.

"How?" Udin asked, spewing a few grains of rice at Atan.

"Err … you finish your dinner. Then we'll go somewhere. Do you know Pak Awang?"

"The Bomoh? Yes," Udin said, licking his fingers. "How much?"

"Huh? How much what?"

"How much will you pay me?" Udin asked, sucking a liquid through a straw from a plastic bag. It was probably iced tea.

"Not me, Pak Awang will pay you," Atan explained.

"OK. Let's go," Udin said. He crumpled up the brown wrapping paper, sucked out the last of the iced tea, leaving the plastic full of little ice cubes, and threw both into the huge monsoon drain behind the bus stop.

"Let's go … err … aren't you going to wash your hand?" Atan pointed at Udin's right hand, which was still stained with curry and a few grains of rice.

Udin looked at his hand, licked each one of his fingers and his thumb, and then wiped his hand on his soiled shirt.

Atan sighed and waved for Udin to follow him to his car.

*****

It was almost midnight, and Atan sat alone in his old car, parked under a huge acacia tree. He had dropped off Awang and Udin at the old cemetery, and now, he presumed that their plans were in motion. Awang and Udin would be digging a grave for the Bangla they called Rocky, and all Atan needed to do was deliver him to the cemetery. As expected, Sue and Rocky came into view. They walked slowly, holding hands, along the village road, oblivious to the fate that awaited them.

*****

Awang waited in the dark with Udin at the entrance of the old cemetery. Udin was sitting close to him. He was afraid. There were numerous ghost stories related to this old cemetery. There were no new graves here, as the piece of land was already congested. The last person to be buried here was a stillborn baby who would have been ten years old by now. Thereafter, the deceased were buried at a bigger piece of land, bequeathed by the government and better-maintained, although many complained it was too far away.

It was half past midnight when Awang heard the clanking and screeching of Atan's old Peugeot. It stopped by the roadside at the entrance. Rocky, all riled up, struggled with the old rusted car door for a few seconds but managed to get himself out the car. He walked into the cemetery while rolling up his sleeves, but immediately he sensed something was wrong. He felt there were others hidden in the darkness. He turned around and saw Atan still in his car, already driving away. Then he saw someone, swinging a shovel, which landed on the left side of his face as he instinctively turned his head. Intense pain flared all over his face as the shovel came down again, smashing his right side.

Udin wanted to hit Rocky one more time, but Awang stopped him. Rocky rocked on his feet for a few seconds and then fell limp on the ground.

"Go dig a hole to bury him," Awang instructed Udin. It dawned on him that they should have dug a hole before Rocky was delivered here.

"Where?" Udin stood there, keeping close to Awang. He was afraid of things in the dark.

"Anywhere …" Awang brushed him off. He was kneeling down next to Rocky. He bent over, trying to see if Rocky was still breathing. Suddenly, Rocky's left hand came up and grabbed Awang's hair. Awang screamed, more in shock than in pain, and clutched both hands around Rocky's throat. He kept the pressure as hard as he could until the hand that was clutching his hair fell back to earth.

Awang caught his breath again. He looked up to see Udin still there, standing near him. "Why are you still standing here? Go dig a hole. We need to hide to body!"

"I … I am scared," Udin said.

Udin's cowardice and lack of urgency angered Awang. "Scared? Scared? You useless, stupid bastard!" Awang got up, grabbed the shovel from Udin's hands, and started swinging it. Udin turned around in horror and started to run, but the shovel caught his buttocks. It stung, and he gave out a cry but kept running away from Awang as fast as his feet could carry him. Instinctively, he ran to Imam Sabri's house, perhaps in search of sanctuary.

Awang was caught in two minds. Should he go after Udin, or should he bury the body? He decided to kill Udin first before he blabbed to someone about their plans. But by the time he got out of the cemetery and onto the road, he realised that his hesitation had given Udin too far a head start. Awang returned to the spot where Rocky was lying, only to find the body gone.

Awang panicked. *God almighty, he's not human,* he thought. *He's come back to life.*

Maybe Udin was right to be afraid. He ran all the way home, got down to the floor, and prostrated himself, asking for forgiveness.

*****

Rocky did not know how long he was unconscious. After the second blow to his face, everything went dark until he awoke and felt somebody's breath on his face. He reached out and grabbed at whatever he could. The person breathing on him screamed and then started to strangle him. He felt too weak to fight back, and he knew he was about to die. He felt sad and lonely. He missed his wife far away in Bangladesh. He felt remorse and deep regret that he had not been true to her. He felt sorry for Sue, for deceiving her and telling her he was unmarried. He missed her too. Maybe he was really in love with her.

He choked as the person tightened his grip on his throat. He let go of whatever his hand was holding onto and was surprised that the person suddenly relaxed his hands on his throat. Then there were some argument. He heard somebody fall on the ground. Somebody screamed, and then he heard footsteps running away, first one set and then another. Everything became quiet. *They are gone,* he thought. He got up to his feet slowly as the world spun around him. He did not know which way to go. He decided to just start walking, his hands in front of him feeling the darkness around him, as he stumbled forward towards what he thought was the main road near the bus stop where he and Sue had rendezvoused just a few hours ago. As he got closer to the light, he let out a sigh of relief. Yes, indeed it was the bus stop. He took another step, and his foot fell onto nothing. He started to fall. His hands flailed to grab onto something, but nothing came to his rescue. His head hit the other side of the concrete monsoon drain, and he lost consciousness again.

*****

Udin banged on the back door of the imam's house, calling out for help. After a few minutes, the door was opened, but the person opening it hid behind the door, revealing the imam with a hunting rifle in his hand, trained on Udin.

Udin squatted down, covering his head. "Don't shoot me!" he screamed. "It's me, Udin. Awang is trying to kill me!" he rushed his explanation.

"What did you do?" ask the good imam.

"Please let me in first, please," Udin begged.

The person behind the door appeared. It was the imam's son. The imam asked his son to drag Udin in. He took one step outside, looked around, and pulled Udin in by one of his arms, which were still resting upon his head.

After Udin told his story, Imam Sabri and his son tied him up so he won't run away. He protested, but the imam threatened to kick him out of the house and he let him deal with Awang himself. Udin gave his hands willingly as the imam's son tied them up. They all then get into the imam's car and drove off to the nearest police station.

Udin confessed everything to the police. The imam and his son went home, and Udin slept in the cell until the police woke him up in the morning to show them where the body was.

At around ten in the morning, a group of policemen came to the old cemetery. Udin was not allowed to get out of the police car. They did not find the body, but there were traces of blood on the ground. They called in the sniffer dogs, and the dogs led them to the monsoon drain.

"They took it away," the old woman sitting at the bus stop said to Inspector Chia, the investigating officer.

"I beg your pardon?" Chia asked.

"The body that was there. Some schoolchildren who were waiting for the bus here early this morning found it. Somebody called the police. They came and took it away," she said.

"Hmm … thank you, Mak Cik," Chia said.

Chia made some calls. Sure enough, a body found in a monsoon drain had been sent to the general hospital in Melaka town for a post-mortem.

Chia then asked Udin to show him where Awang lived. He was sure Awang would be far away by now. But to his surprise, there he was in the kitchen, prostrating himself and crying. He muttered something that sounded like, "Please forgive me, please forgive me."

Chia walked in and tapped Awang on his back. Awang was startled. At first, he thought of running, but there was nowhere to run.

"Will you come with me to the police station, please, sir?" Chia said carefully, suspecting that Awang might not be mentally stable. Awang gave out a sigh. He held out his hands out for Chia to handcuff.

Awang and Udin both sat in the backseat on the way to the police station. Atan joined them later that day.

A Sacrifice for
the Bridge

Udin was not crazy. He was a little slow, maybe.

The first time we actually met, I was really annoyed. I was having breakfast at my usual *mamak* restaurant when he came in and decided to sit with me at my table. I had seen him before, meandering up and down the street in front of my office building. But I would just ignore him as we passed each other, turning my sight away from him and pretending I did notice him. I noticed that he would always ask whoever was looking at him for money by holding his right hand close to his chest and rubbing his index figure against his thumb. If you nodded your head, only then would he approach you and ask for two ringgit.

That morning, I was reading my newspaper when suddenly, Udin sat at my table and ordered iced tea. The waitress smiled at him and, a few moments later, brought him his order. I would not have minded sharing my table with anybody, but I wondered when Udin last had a bath. He stank, and I was sitting downwind from a wall fan that wafted his odour directly toward me.

He asked me something I could not catch. It was something about the women sitting at a few tables behind me. I turned my head to have a look and a breath of fresh air and saw that the women were my office mates. He continued mumbling.

From what little I could gather, he was interested in one particular person at the table. She was one of my staff. I told him she was a married woman. He finished his drink, paid the waitress, and left. His scent, however, lingered.

The next morning I had breakfast with another colleague. As we were discussing office politics, he suddenly got up and called out Udin's name. Udin was on the other side of the street. He turned his head towards us and waved at my friend. My friend waved back, beckoning him to come over.

Udin looked different. He had gotten a haircut, and his hair was combed neatly. He was wearing a clean red T-shirt and a pair of slacks. For a homeless person eating sparsely (I presume, although I never saw him eat), he had a rather plump physique. He crossed the street, sat at our table, and ordered iced tea. My friend teased him about his appearance that morning and he mumbled something about trying to get a job. My friend laughed and wished him luck. He finished his drink and stood up to pay. My friend told him he was buying and gave Udin a five-ringgit note, and Udin left.

My friend shook his head and said he pitied Udin. I said, "No need to pity a crazy person; they are happier than us." My friend did not laugh at my joke. He then started to tell Udin's story.

Udin never knew his father. His mother did not want to talk about him. He grew up alone in a rented house just outside Muar town. His mother worked as a waitress at a coffee shop in Muar. When Udin was a baby, an elderly neighbour offered to take care of him while his mother was at work, but just as he started to walk, the old woman died. Udin's mother could not find another babysitter who would take care of Udin, at least not one that she could afford. So she made an arrangement with the coffee shop owner to let Udin stay in an upstairs room, which eventually she made her home.

Udin was easy to care for. He slept most of the time, cried when hungry, and would sleep again once fed. As his mother tended tables downstairs, he would either be sleeping upstairs or sitting at a table at the back of the shop just watching his mother scurry around the coffee shop, taking orders and cleaning up the tables. She was good at her job, fast and efficient so that the shop owner was tolerant of Udin's benign presence.

As he grew up, his mother realised that Udin had some learning disorder. Even after he had finished standard three of the primary school, he was still struggling with his reading and writing, although he was good at arithmetic. Socially, he was a loner. He mumbled when he talked, making him difficult to understand. Most people didn't mind having him around, simply because he would eventually fade into the background and later be totally forgotten.

By the time he finished standard six, his mother saw that he would not be able to cope with the lessons in secondary school or the peer pressure of the teenage world. She believed Udin needed to be constantly under her radar. So, she did not register him for secondary school. Instead, she asked Udin to hang around the coffee shop and help her with her chores.

The coffee shop owner was a little apprehensive, afraid of being accused of condoning child labour, but later saw how useful Udin was. His arithmetic skills helped when calculating the bills and adding up customer's orders quickly. Udin even became a sort of sideshow to the customers, when he would be asked to take the orders and say what the customer's total bill would be, there and then. Some even tipped him for his performance.

Things went well for a few years. His mother and he became a fixture to the coffee shop, she for her efficient customer service and Udin for his mental-arithmetic prowess.

Then, one morning, Udin woke up and could not find his mother. On her bed, Udin found a note and a butter cookies tin can. He gave the note to the coffee shop owner when he came to open the shop at dawn. The coffee shop owner, after reading the note, had to find a place to sit down.

"To Uncle Lim," the note began. "I know Udin would give this note to you since he could not read very well.

"Uncle Lim, I know you have warned me before, but I can't help myself. My husband came back last month, and, well, it looks like I am pregnant again. I must really love him, because he kept lying to me and I believe him each time. He said he would be a better husband to me and spend equal time between me and his first wife in Kuala Lumpur. He said he would send me money more often. But Uncle Lim, he only comes back when he has a fight with his first wife. He badmouths her, telling me what a terrible wife she is and saying that he will soon divorce her. He said she knows about me, but I doubt it. Uncle Lim, I called him to let him know that I am pregnant again, and he asked me to abort. He said I did it before, when I was pregnant after I had Udin. But I did not tell him that I did not kill our second child. I gave birth to a beautiful baby girl, cut the umbilical cord myself, and put her in a box in front of a mosque. I saw a nice man take her home. She has a good home.

"I cannot bear to kill a child, nor can I afford to let this unborn child live. Udin is big enough to take care of himself. Just let him work around the shop, and give him what you paid me. He will be better off without me. The world will be better off without me. Don't look for me. I hear the bridge has not had its annual sacrifice this year.

"Take care of yourself and Udin," the letter ended.

Uncle Lim pulled Udin close, hugged him, and cried. Udin did not understand and asked where his mother was. Uncle Lim said she had gone to meet someone and it would be some time before she came back. "I'll take care of you," Uncle Lim said.

Uncle Lim read in the newspaper the next day about a woman who asked for a taxi to Tanjung Gading, across the river from Muar town. She asked the taxi driver to stop at the top of the Muar Bridge, climbed over the railings, and disappeared beneath the murky water of the Muar River.

Udin continued to work at Uncle Lim's coffee shop until Uncle Lim himself passed away. Uncle Lim had only one child. His son was educated in the UK and was later employed in Singapore. The shop was sold to a relative, who rented it out to a fast-food franchise. The whole block was later turned into a budget hotel, with the exception of one small laundry shop.

Udin lived off the money his mother left him and his own savings while working for Uncle Lim. When the coffee shop was sold to the franchise, he became homeless, sleeping anywhere he could as long no one chased him away. When his money ran out, he started to beg.

"He's not crazy, my friend. He just doesn't know what to do. All his life, someone would tell him when to wake up, when to sleep, and when to bathe. Now he just walks around town. I heard he does ask for his mother sometimes," my friend said, finishing his story of Udin.

Thereafter, each day as part of my ritual in preparing myself for work, I would ensure I had some change in my wallet just in case I bumped into Udin. When I did see him, he would meekly show two fingers at me, but I would always give him five ringgit. Then one day he just disappeared.

Printed in the United States
By Bookmasters